SAFI, AND THE GOD OF DEATH

Ashri Gyorgi

13HORROR.COM BOOKS
An imprint of
DIZZY EMU PUBLISHING
1714 N McCadden Place, Hollywood, Los Angeles 90028
dizzyemupublishing.com

Safi, and the God of Death
Ashri Gyorgi

First published in the United States
in 2022 by 13Horror.com Books

SAFI, AND THE GOD OF DEATH

Ashri Gyorgi

SUPERIMPOSE, OVER BLACK: "The old world is dying, and the new
world struggles to be born; now is the time of monsters."
- Antonio Gramsci

                                                  FADE IN:

INT. AMARS' HOUSE, SYRIA - NIGHT

YOUNG SAFI'S POV: illuminated by a kerosine lamp, an old
picture book with drawings in Aztec style comes into view.

                    TAHA (O.S.)
                (reads in English)
          From the void, the first god,
          Ometeotl created themselves -- both
          male and female, good and evil,
          light and darkness. Ometeotl
          birthed four main gods:
          Quetzalcoatl, the god of wind and
          visions, Huitzilopochtli, the god
          of war and peace, Tezcatlipoca, the
          god of judgement and night, and
          Xipe Totec, the god of rebirth.

REVERSE: YOUNG SAFI (7), precocious and button-cute with
olive skin, is curled up in bed, her head on the shoulder of
TAHA AMAR (late 30s), sophisticated and brawny with thick-
lens glasses. Her father, reading a "bedtime story."

From the brief glimpses we get, it's clear that their home is
modest and shabby -- but imbued with a cozy sense of warmth.

They speak Arabic with subtitles:

                    TAHA (CONT'D)
          According to the Aztecs, there were
          four other worlds before ours...
          and each of those worlds was
          destroyed by warring gods --

He turns the page to a picture of Xolotl, an imposing being
with a dog's face.

                    YOUNG SAFI
          He looks just like Anubis!

                    TAHA
          Oh, yes! There's a connection
          between our ancestors and the
          Olmecs, the Aztecs, and the Maya.

He kisses her forehead, gets up.

                    TAHA (CONT'D)
          It's complicated. But maybe you'll
          figure it out when you grow up!

He extinguishes the lamp. Safi drifts off to sleep as Taha
leaves the room. A beat, then --

                                        ENTER DREAM
                                        SEQUENCE:

In the distance, the majestic Nile sparkles under the sun.

Dressed like an ancient Egyptian child, young Safi runs
through the lush, sun-speckled greenery, following
semitransparent WISPS OF GOLDEN PARTICLES spreading like
smoke through the air.

She slows down at a wondrous sight:

Amidst an ethereal haze, a GIANT ALIEN (golden and iridescent
blue, of uncertain gender - heavily muscled, but with
breasts, with a birdlike beak of a nose) lumbers forward. A
towering spaceship idles behind him.

He walks up to her, leans in. His eyes, dotted with MULTIPLE
IRISES, peer at her face inquisitively, as he smiles and
caresses her cheek.

                                        CUT BACK TO:

INT. AMARS' KITCHEN - MORNING

A meager affair; all earthen walls, a wood stove, and worn-
down cookware. Taha, young Safi, and her mother ZAFIRA (30s),
lithe and spirited, sit at a table, drinking tea with Syrian
pita bread.

                        TAHA (CONT'D)
                ... What a marvelous dream, Safi!
                It's the exact same one your uncle
                Abdul used to have as a child!
                Incredible. It may have something
                to do with our past. The ancestors
                of Druze *did* come from Egypt...

                        ZAFIRA
                Don't fill up her head with that
                superstitious nonsense now. She has
                to focus on the real world.

                        TAHA
                    (agreeable, nodding)
                Yes, of course. Forget what I said,
                Safi.

A beat. Then, Taha WINKS conspiratorially at Safi. She
smiles.

INT./EXT. OLD SEDAN - DRIVING - NIGHT

SUPER: 'MEXICO, EIGHT YEARS LATER'

Grown SAFI AMAR (15), a spunky tom-boy with cropped hair, is
driving alone down a rural road. She reaches to the littered
passenger seat, grabs a packet of jerky, pulls out a piece
and throws it in her mouth.

Chewing, she scans the road signs. Slowing down, she then
turns into a small parking lot.

EXT./INT. SMALL HOTEL - NIGHT

Her old, banged up sedan parks awkwardly in one of the slots
in front of a building with a sign: "$30/night."

Safi looks warily at the hotel's fluorescent-lit windows,
exits the car, heads to the entrance.

Inside, ADELA (70s), a grandmotherly Native woman with kind
eyes, looks up as Safi walks to the counter.

                    SAFI
              (slight Arabic accent)
          Thirty dollars for a room?

She counts out the cash on the counter.

                    ADELA
              (Spanish accent)
          It's forty for two beds.

                    SAFI
          I need only one.

                    ADELA
          Aren't you a bit too young to
          travel alone?

                    SAFI
          I'm eighteen! I just have a baby-
          face.

                    ADELA
          I have four teenage grand-kids,
          mija. You're fifteen, at most. Are
          you a runaway?

Safi shakes her head, not looking at Adela.

                    ADELA (CONT'D)
          There are a lot of bad people
          around. Especially when you're a
          young girl traveling alone.

Safi takes this in. Off her plaintive expression, we --

                              ENTER FLASHBACK:

INT. GROUP HOME - DAY

Safi (hair longer) and THREE OTHER KIDS (different ages) sit
at a battered table. TRISH (40s) dour, white, and portly,
with a large crucifix necklace, ladles greasy stew from a
pressure cooker pot into bowls.

Her husband CARL (40s), a balding meat-head, distributes
bread to the kids.

Safi tastes the soup gingerly, then involuntarily makes a gag
face. Trish notices.

                    TRISH
          Not up to your standards, honey?
          Well, sorry I don't run a five-star
          restaurant here. Oughta still be
          better than some smelly Arab grub
          at the refugee camp, though.

                    CARL
          Go easy on the new girl, Trish.
          She's a fragile little thing. Ain't
          you, doll?

Carl winks lecherously at Safi. She looks quickly away. Her
eyes stop at -- A BREAD KNIFE on the table.

                              END FLASHBACK.

Safi looks up at Adela.

                    SAFI
          There's bad people everywhere.

                    ADELA
             (sighs)
          They all seem to crawl out of their
          holes these days.
             (beat)
          Where are your parents?

                    SAFI
          .. In Colorado.
             (beat)
          They have, like, important jobs, so
          they couldn't come with me.

                    ADELA
          Did they get you that car?

                    SAFI
          (nods)
     And some money for the trip. I'm
     just going to see the museum
     tomorrow, and then driving...
          (beat)
     Back home, to... Colorado!

                    ADELA
     You must be mature for your age,
     that they let you go alone.
          (beat, smiles)
     My son's in Texas. He's bringing
     his family tomorrow, for the
     festival.

Adela gives Safi a card room key.

                    ADELA (CONT'D)
     Stop by in the morning before you
     leave. I don't serve breakfast, but
     I'll have something for you.

                    SAFI
          (nods)
     Gracias!

Safi walks down the corridor, reaches her door, unlocks it,
hesitates, looks back at Adela wistfully -- just as a PHONE
RINGS on her desk:

Adela answers, coos in a mix of English and Spanish. Some
words reach Safi:

                    ADELA (O.S.)
     I'll see you tomorrow, *mi cielo*...
     And a nice fresh Flan! You tell
     your mother to watch her own
     weight, my *precioso*!?

Safi turns away, sad, walks into the room.

INT. HOTEL ROOM - LATER

Unremarkable, but clean enough. Safi's nice, traditional
shirt is spread out on a chair. In bed, she browses the same
book about Aztecs that Taha used to read to her.

Safi looks at a photo that serves as a placeholder: a
Polaroid taken at the refugee camp, of herself, a couple
years younger, and her parents.

She peers at it as we --

                                        ENTER FLASHBACK:

INT. AMARS' TENT - NIGHT

Taha, Safi, and Zafira sit on the floor of a bare-bones tent, eating. They speak in Arabic, with subtitles.

                    TAHA
          One day, we'll live in a nice
          house, in a peaceful, quiet place.
               (to Safi)
          Your mom will go back to school and
          become a nurse. Maybe even a
          doctor!

Zafira, pouring coffee, SCOFFS.

                    ZAFIRA
          A doctor! Cleaning lady in a
          hospital, if I'm lucky!

                    TAHA
               (to Safi)
          Always pretends she has no
          ambition, as if we don't know her!

                    SAFI
          And you, dad? Who will you be?

                    TAHA
          Oh, I'm not sure... Someone's got
          to work.

                    SAFI
          I mean, if you could be anything
          you wanted to be?!

                    TAHA
               (dreamy expression)
          I suppose an archeologist. And I
          would take you with me everywhere I
          can. And we would travel too, as a
          family. We'd see Tenochtitlan, and
          Mitla, and Abydos... everything!

Safi grins broadly.

                              END FLASHBACK.

Safi puts the book away, lies back, closes her eyes. A few
beats. Then, gradually --

A light TAP-TAP-TAP of steps in the corridor becomes audible.
Almost like a goat prancing past. It's followed by weird
HISSING WHISPERS, also from outside the door and then --

A MUFFLED SCREAM.

Safi's head bolts up from the pillow. Startled, she gets to
her feet and heads cautiously for the door.

INT. HOTEL CORRIDOR - CONTINUOUS

Safi tiptoes out of the room, checks the empty, dark
corridor. The LIGHTS FLICKER ABOVE...

A SLURPING SOUND can be distantly heard.

                    SAFI
          Hello?

No response. Safi creeps along the corridor, sees --

A CLEANING CART parked by the turn. The slurping grows
louder. She approaches it, peeks from behind the corner. And
her eyes go SAUCER-SIZED upon seeing --

The shimmering skeletal form of a female Aztec demon,
TZITZIMIMEH, hunched and wraithlike, eyeballs glistening in
its gnarled skull face, as it kneels before ADELA'S CORPSE.

The poor woman's chest has been torn open as the demonic
entity gorges itself on her still-pumping HEART.

Frozen in terror, Safi steps backwards only to stumble
noisily into the cart. It OVERTURNS as she falls to the
ground. Shaking herself off, she glances up to find --

The Tzitzimimeh's ghastly SKULL now right in front of her
face, CHITTERING its rotted teeth madly. Safi SCREAMS.
Instinct takes hold, so she reaches out and punches it!

The Tzitzimimeh SCREAMS like a banshee, then POUNCES as we --

                                        SLAM TO:

INT. HOTEL ROOM - MORNING

Safi wakes up, with a GASP, only to discover herself in bed.
She gets up, hurries to the door, and pokes her head out --

SAFI'S POV: Unharmed, Adela works at the front desk.

Safi EXHALES in relief, closes the door, walks to the window.
Still shaken, she opens the curtains to look outside.

SAFI'S POV: the sleepy town of Mitla is waking up. A LONE
SHOP OWNER drags out a stand with plastic skeletons hanging.

                                        ENTER MONTAGE:

1) As the sun rises, so too do the people of Mitla. They
begin buzzing about preparing for a DAY OF THE DEAD
celebration.

2) WOMEN adorn sugar skulls for sale; shops and houses are
decorated with La Catrina, skeletons, and other icons of
death and the underworld.

3) TOURISTS roam the streets, snapping photos.

EXT./INT. ACOSTA'S SHOP - DAY

In the glass storefront of a humble shop, a small 'orchestra'
of mechanized skeletons plays a Mexican tune.

Inside, a great variety of Halloween and the Day Of The Dead
paraphernalia sprawls out through the aisles. We GLIDE
through the space as NOISE emanates from the back, THINGS
DRAGGED AROUND, DROPPED, BANGING.

ISOBEL (70s), high strung and still a beauty, hurries out of
that area, searching frantically on and under the counters.

Finally, she calls out, exasperated:

                    ISOBEL
              (in Spanish, subtitled)
          Alejandro?! I can't find the truck
          keys anywhere!

ALEJANDRO (70s), a ringer for Wes Studi, with a regal
bearing, walks in from the back toting an armful of hangable
dummies with painted death masks. He watches his frazzled
wife as she searches.

                    ISOBEL (CONT'D)
          I don't know what I've done with
          them! Again!
              (almost crying)
          My memory's shot! Old and stupid,
          and growing dumber by the day!

                    ALEJANDRO
              (scoffs)
          Old?! Slow down, darling!

He puts the dummies down, gazes around.

                    ISOBEL
          I was sure I left them by the
          register!

Alejandro smiles as we enter his --

OTHERWORLDLY POV: his vision glows, penetrating through objects like an X-ray until it locates a bunch of keys under a pile of frightful masks in the corner.

He narrows his eyes at the keys and, totally unbeknownst to Isobel, they 'float' behind her back, straight to the register.

NOTE: as we will come to learn, Alejandro is, in fact, the Aztec god XOLOTL living a mortal life among humans

                    ALEJANDRO/XOLOTL
          Maybe you overlooked them?

She GRUNTS, marches to the register. He follows.

                    ISOBEL
          I checked there already!

She perfunctorily checks underneath some piles of papers. But then, as she shuts the register's open lower drawer --

The keys 'hiding' underneath is revealed!

                    ISOBEL (CONT'D)
          Hostia! How did I miss them?!

                    ALEJANDRO/XOLOTL
          You were in too much of a rush. As
          usual.

He makes a show of SNIFFING her like a dog.

                    ALEJANDRO/XOLOTL (CONT'D)
          Mmmm... You're not old in the
          slightest, _hermosa_!

She GIGGLES like a schoolgirl, jokingly pushes him away.

                    ISOBEL
          Come on, you big hound, before you
          make yourself late!

EXT. THE ACOSTA'S SHOP/INT. ALEJANDRO'S TRUCK - CONTINUOUS

Isobel and Alejandro put the dummies into the already overstuffed trailer of a large, old, cargo truck. He shuts the trailer door, kisses her.

                    ISOBEL
          Go make us some _moolah_ --
               (slaps his bum)
          You sexy devil!

He climbs into the driver's seat, shuts the door, smiling.

                    ALEJANDRO/XOLOTL
                         (sotto)
               Right on both accounts. A devil.
               And a sexy one!

He sticks the key in the ignition, but the truck just WHEEZES
impotently. He glances at the rear view mirror, spotting
Isobel, watching anxiously.

He pulls the key out, drops it on the passenger seat, peers
at the switch. A HELLFIRE FLICKERS IN HIS EYES, AND --

The truck starts! In the rear view mirror, Isobel smiles,
relieved, waves farewell.

Alejandro drives off, WHISTLING A TUNE.

EXT. 'ENTRANCE TO THE UNDERWORLD' - LATER

A recreation of the Grand Hall of Columns looms large outside
MITLA'S MUSEUM as TOURISTS form lines to enter.

                                        ENTER MONTAGE:

1) We enter the museum ahead of the tourists. For this small
town, its surprisingly sprawling and impressively detailed.

2) ROOM UPON ROOM lined with Aztec artifacts -- smaller
replicas of temples built to fit into some of the rooms. Some
of them are a bit shopworn.

3) In the museum's shop, A CLERK accepts from Alejandro a box
with death masks and the like.

4) Alejandro and XANA (late 20s) a lithe and tan young woman,
helps WORKERS to cart and set up displays -- ghouls, coffins,
demons, most with Aztec motifs.

                                        END MONTAGE.

INT. MUSEUM - CONTINUOUS

Xana turns to Alejandro.

                    XANA
               You don't know how much we
               appreciate this!

                    ALEJANDRO/XOLOTL
               Thank me after you turn a profit.

                    XANA
               That shouldn't be a problem, right?

                    ALEJANDRO/XOLOTL
          Combining the Day of the Dead with
          the Halloween? I think you'll end
          up in the black. The kids will eat
          it up.

The slovenly janitor, ENRIQUE (50), stumbles drunkenly past
them with a broom, pushing a splashing bucket of dirty water.

                    XANA
          Would be nice to afford a security
          update, and --
                    (re: Enrique, sotto)
          Maybe, some new personnel.
                    (at the displays)
          Still. These busted old things
          cheapen it, don't you think?

Making sure he's not observed by the workers and Enrique,
Alejandro turns to some of the more frayed displays and --

Makes some small movements with his hands as HELLFIRE subtly
flickers in his eyes. Within instants, THEY MEND AND SPRUCE
UP THEMSELVES. He and Xana share a conspiratorial smile.

NOTE: We will come to learn that Xana is, in fact, the
immortal goddess Xonaxi posing in human form.

                    ALEJANDRO/XOLOTL
          Safer than to use magic to rob
          banks.

                    XANA/XONAXI
          You would know... Do you remember
          the archbishop coming all the way
          out here to perform his exorcisms?
          That didn't end too well.

They CHUCKLE. Alejandro picks up a box, but drops it with a
small GROAN of pain. He straightens up, rubs his lower back,
winces. Xana watches, fascinated and repulsed.

                    XANA/XONAXI (CONT'D)
          Do you ever regret giving up your
          immortality?

                    ALEJANDRO/XOLOTL
          I don't want to stay young while
          she grows old. And I don't want to
          spend an eternity missing her after
          she's gone.

                    XANA/XONAXI
          How romantic. Misguided, but
          romantic all the same.

                    ALEJANDRO/XOLOTL
          Maybe one day, tomorrow, or
          centuries from now, you'll meet
          someone and understand.

                    XANA/XONAXI
          You really think this world will
          last that long?

EXT. THE MUSEUM - VISITOR'S QUEUE - CONTINUOUS

A New Mexico Pueblo High School Soccer Team takes up much of
the line. The TEENS are LOUD, horse-playing and generally
causing a ruckus. Among them are --

RAFA, an ADHD troublemaker, ANTONIO, stout and stern, BLY, a
skinny spaz, CHAD, handsome and dull, DONALD, peppy and
manic, SCOTTY, pimple-faced and insecure, ERIC, nasty and
overly hostile, and CALIAN, the captain, tall, strapping.

We land on ANAYA, model looks, lots of makeup, kitty-ears
headband keeping her long hair tamed, the school's lead
cheerleader, as she clings to her boyfriend Calian.

Also in the queue, behind Anaya and Calian, is MS. ROMERO
(40), Native American, the group's chaperone and Rafa's mom,
with Rafa's curious siblings MARTIN (6) and MONIQUE (8)
followed by --

Safi, with her backpack, looking as cleaned up as her
situation allows. She registers as a bit out of place.

                    MS. ROMERO
               (at Safi's shirt)
          What a beautiful blouse!

                    SAFI
          It's a Kesrewan pattern --

                    MS. ROMERO
          A what-now? Are you an Arab?

Anaya and Calian turn, eye Safi. Her and Calian's eyes meet.
He smiles to her, sure of his charms -- which do work on her.

                    SAFI
               (lies)
          We... immigrated from Egypt.

                    CALIAN
          Wow! That's so cool. Did you live
          near the Pyramids?

Anaya makes a face, jealous.

                    SAFI
              (on a roll)
     Um... Sure, not far. My mom's a
     doctor. And my dad's an
     archeologist. He knows a lot about
     Aztecs, and Mayas, and the
     pharaohs.

                    MS. ROMERO
     Impressive! Are they here with you?

                    SAFI
     Yeah... But they decided to check
     the town first, and I wanted to see
     the museum.

Just then, Bly sneaks over to Anaya, pulls the kitty ears
headband from her hair, sticks it on his own head, and runs
away, LAUGHING. She takes off after him.

                    CALIAN
              (after Bly, chuckling)
     Bly, baby, you look sexy!

To prevent Ms Romero from asking her any more questions:

                    SAFI
     Where are _you_ guys from?

                    MS. ROMERO
     New Mexico. Our soccer team had a
     scrimmage here.

                    SAFI
     Are you their coach?

                    MS. ROMERO
     Oh, heavens no. The coach used the
     opportunity to visit some
     relatives. I teach history, but my
     oldest's on the team so I
     volunteered as a chaperon.

She nods at Rafa.

                    MS. ROMERO (CONT'D)
     I brought my sprouts too.
              (to Martin and Monique)
     Say hi to...

She stares at Safi inquiringly. Safi smiles at the kids.

                    SAFI
     I'm Safi. What are your names?

                    MARTIN   MONIQUE
Martin!   Monique!

NOISE AND LAUGHTER break out ahead of them as they see Rafa
wrestling with Bly, who GASPS for air in Rafa's choke-hold,
while Anaya tries to pull her headband off his head.

                         MS. ROMERO
                    (barks)
               Rafa! Bly!
                    (sarcastic)
               Sorry to interrupt your little love
               embrace!

The rest of the group SNICKER. Anaya snatches her headband
from Bly's head. Rafa releases him.

                         RAFA
               Can we skip the museum, mom... I
               mean, Ms. Romero? Maybe we could
               try some of that fried ice cream
               downtown instead?!

                         MS. ROMERO
               You can have some fun after you
               learn something, for a change.

                         RAFA
               Why do we have to learn about
               stupid Aztecs?! They're not our
               ancestors! We don't have squat to
               do with their wacko religion!

                         SAFI
                    (butting in, incensed)
               Oh, yeah, like what do you think
               Kachinas signify?!

Ms. Romero smiles, intrigued.

                         MS. ROMERO
               Why don't you enlighten us, Safi?

                         SAFI
                    (showing off)
               Kachinas replaced the sacrificial
               victims, as proxies of the gods. So
               now, to communicate with a god,
               instead of a blood sacrifice,
               people use his Kachina ritual!

                         MS. ROMERO
               How impressive!

                    RAFA
          (to his friends, at Safi)
     Stuck-up know it all!

                    ANAYA
          (to Rafa, sotto)
     Rich Arab thinks she's better than
     us!
          (mocks Safi's accent)
     'Oooh, my mother is a doctor! My
     father is an archeologist!'

The friends make faces, talk in low voices, LAUGH. Behind,
Safi listens uncomfortably.

EXT./INT. CURATOR'S OFFICE - CONTINUOUS

A plaque on the door reads: 'Employees only.'

We float through the darkened room before landing on --

The bony, ghoulish face of MICTLAN, the Aztec God of Death.
It's carved on a sand-stone container. In a terrarium at the
base of the bust, pet beetles crawl over bones of some poor
rodent as they pick its flesh clean.

Xana and Alejandro carry in some extra decorations and pile
them in a corner.

Alejandro stops in front of the shelf hosting various
figurines, and stares at Mictlan's container. Xana stops
besides him.

                    ALEJANDRO/XOLOTL
          You think he's aware of what's
          going on around him?

                    XANA/XONAXI
          Maybe, like in a dream?

MICTLAN'S POV: Xana's and Alejandro's silhouettes stare back
at him through a thick haze, distorted as if seen via fish-
eye lens. Their voices reach him distantly:

                    ALEJANDRO/XOLOTL
          He might try again. The New Fire's
          getting close.

                    XANA/XONAXI
          It'll be over in a week.

                    ALEJANDRO/XOLOTL
          Long enough for him to wreck havoc.
               (beat)
          Remember 1819?!

                    XANA
          He's not on display anymore, is
          he?! Don't worry so much.
               (pointed glance at his
               body)
          You might get ulcers.

INT. MUSEUM - MAIN SPACE - CONTINUOUS

The crowd of TOURISTS enter the large glass entrance into the
main part of the museum.

Safi stops and examines one of the exhibits: an intimidating
ORNATE KNIFE IN A GLASS CASE.

                                        QUICK FLASH:

Taha shows her an illustration in the book of the same knife.

                    TAHI
          ... The priests used it to cut open
          the chests of the tributes. Only
          one genuine Tecpatl was ever found
          remaining.

                                        BACK TO:

As the Pueblo soccer team, including Calian, Rafa, and Anaya,
Ms. Romero, Monique and Martin, followed by Safi, pass by the
curator's office's door --

INT. CURATOR OFFICE - CONTINUOUS

Through the darkness of the empty office --

MICTLAN POV: through his container/figurine, like X-Ray
vision, he spies A GLOWING WISP OF GOLDEN PARTICLES waft
through the cracks around the door... reaching his shelf...

After a beat, the figurine GLOWS, then twitches once as if
awoken... before going still once more.

INT. MUSEUM - CONTINUOUS

Along the way, the teens gawk at displays, interspersed with
a few Halloween and the Day Of the Dead decorations.

DONALD wanders close to a dummy of an EVIL CLOWN. It GROWLS
and its claw-like hand grabs Donald's shoulder. Donald
SCREAMS, Anaya SQUEALS.

                    ERIC (O.S.)
          Got you!

Eric sticks out from behind the monster, moving its arms like
a puppeteer.

                    DONALD
               (chases Eric)
          Fuck you, dude!

Everybody LAUGHS.

                    MS. ROMERO
          Hey! Behave yourselves! Come on,
          the presentation is about to start!

INT. DISPLAY ROOM 1 - MOMENTS LATER

Various Aztec artifacts in glass cases. Some VISITORS browse
the displays. Others, including the Pueblo teens, listen:

                    KIKI (O.S.)
          ... Quetzalcoatl convinced the gods
          to retire to their spirit realm.

Safi wanders closer to the crowd surrounding KIKI (20s), seen
from the back, a measured indigenous Mexican, with long,
flowing black hair.

                    KIKI (O.S.) (CONT'D)
          Humankind has matured enough to
          rely on itself, he said... and
          instead of giving their life-force
          to the gods...

A slide projected onto the large screen: PRIESTS performing
bloody sacrifices to HUITZILOPOCHTLI'S IDOL, presented as a
birdlike figure coated in resplendent blue and yellow
stripes, armed with his magical sword XIUHCOATL.

                    KIKI (SEEN FROM THE BACK) (CONT'D)
          Humans should serve their fellow
          men through good deeds. But
          Mictlantecutli, the god of death
          and the ruler of the Underworld,
          didn't fall in line.

Slide: In the UNDERWORLD, the god MICTLAN -- a likeness with
the image on the stone container -- munches hungrily on human
flesh scraps falling from the gods' feasting table.

                    KIKI (O.S.) (CONT'D)
          He pretended to be Quetzalcoatl and
          instructed Montezuma to continue
          the sacrifices --

Slide: Spectral Mictlan whispers to sleeping MONTEZUMA.

> KIKI (O.S.) (CONT'D)
> Promising to grant him victories
> over his enemies.

Slide: War CAPTIVES are sacrificed by the PRIESTS --

> KIKI (O.S.) (CONT'D)
> More and more people were
> sacrificed, but the hunger and
> plagues grew, until, at last, the
> Aztec empire fell.

Slide: SPANISH CONQUISTADORS execute MONTEZUMA.

> KIKI (O.S.) (CONT'D)
> Charged with power from the vast
> amounts of blood, Mictlan was at
> his strongest, and ready to devour
> the entire world.

Slide: In the underworld, Mictlan feasts upon a huge pile of
human hearts, growing fat and contented from the orgy of gory
consumption.

> KIKI (O.S.) (CONT'D)
> And he would have succeeded, were
> it not for his two wives, who hated
> him for forcing them into
> servitude...

> ENTER ANIMATED
> RE-ENACTMENT:

INT. THE UNDERWORLD

1. In murky, dank darkness, heavily pregnant XONAXI (who we
recognize as Xana, but clad in Aztec goddess attire) and her
brother/sister COQUI -- an androgynous 'two spirit' male --
set about dismembering corpses.

> KIKI (V.O.)
> ... They conspired with
> Quetzalcoatl and Huitzilopochtli,
> the brother gods, to trick Mictlan--

2. The wives hold fast a glowing container that shakes and
rumbles, threatening to pop out of their hands, but finally
grows cold and still.

> KIKI (V.O. - CONT'D)
> -- and trapped him in a stone
> figurine.

Xonaxi and Coqui smile in relief to each other above it.

BACK TO:

The museum, where Anaya raises her hand. The rest of the kids goof off behind Ms. Romero's back.

>   ANAYA
>   (to Kiki)
>   Why would Mictlan want to destroy
>   our world?!

Kiki is REVEALED/seen from the front:

They are none other is _Coqui, Mictlan's wife and Xonaxi's co-conspirator, dressed in modern clothing_. A curator's name tag on their shirt reads 'Kiki.'

>   KIKI/COQUI
>   Once the humans were dead and the
>   fifth sun was gone, he hoped to
>   turn the whole world into his dark
>   kingdom, inhabited by monsters
>   worshipping him. He, a minor god,
>   would become a supreme ruler of the
>   universe!
>   (beat)
>   Pretty cool for the bastard, huh?

INT. CURATOR'S OFFICE - DAY

A KEY IS HEARD TURNING in the lock. Enrique pushes his cart inside, closes the door, turns on a flashlight. From the shelf, Mictlan's stone face peers out impassively as:

Enrique removes a tile on the wall, extracts a hidden bottle of tequila, and takes a few lusty sips. Then, he freezes upon hearing:

>   OTHERWORLDLY WHISPER (O.S.)
>   (distant, quiet)
>   Riches and power...
>   (close and closer)
>   Riches and power... Boys or
>   girls...
>   (right next to him)
>   Anything you want, can be yours...

Enrique SHRIEKS, BUMPS into the shelf, dropping the flashlight and the bottle. The shelf's contents RATTLE and Mictlan's container falls into --

The terrarium, illuminated by the flashlight on the floor. It CRACKS upon impact, releasing a small puff of green SMOKE which envelops the nearest BEETLE.

The beetle convulses, then steadies itself, opens its wings
and rises above his feasting brothers.

                    BEETLE/MICTLAN
          Enrique! My good man!

Enrique falls to his knees, watching the terrarium. He
crosses himself, hypnotized, his mouth open in wonder as the
beetle slowly ascends above the terrarium's wall and hovers.

                    BEETLE/MICTLAN (CONT'D)
          Let's get acquainted.

The beetle suddenly darts into Enrique's open mouth! Enrique
grabs his throat, eyes bulging. He makes a CHOKING SOUND as
the whites of his eyes go black and we --

                                        SLAM TO:

INT. FRONT LOBBY - CONTINUOUS

The area is deserted, as the tourists' group has passed into
the interior. Xana checks the exhibits and decorations. She
stops short by the knife's display, gapes upon finding:

The glass case is broken, the ceremonial knife is missing.
Stunned, she turns around only to --

Come FACE TO FACE with Enrique/Mictlan, standing *right behind
her*, blackened eyes staring into her soul.

                    XANA
          What the --

He blows green smoke into her face, which flutters into her
mouth and nostrils.

She wavers, grabs her throat just as Enrique did before...
the whites of her eyes go black as she stares at:

Enrique, back to normal, gaping in bewilderment.

                    ENRIQUE
          How did I get here?
            (beat, looks down)
          What the hell is this?..

He looks at the knife, Tecpatl, in his hands. Xana/Mictlan
exhales, eyes returning to normal. She smiles.

                    XANA/MICTLAN
          I'll take that, thank you!

Xana/Mictlan takes the knife and, in one fell swoop, SLASHES
ENRIQUE'S CHEST OPEN. Enrique drops with a deathly GASP.

Xana/Mictlan reaches into his open chest cavity and scoops
out his heart with a sickening *THWACK*. She holds it up to her
lips and takes a big BITE. Tastes it, makes a face.

                    XANA/MICTLAN (CONT'D)
               Bitter with an impending stroke...
               Still, it does hit the spot.

She swallows it like a python swallowing a frog.

INT. ROOM 1 - CONTINUOUS

Calian questions Kiki:

                    CALIAN
               ... But wouldn't other gods stop
               him?

                    KIKI/COQUI
               The gods had passed out of this
               realm. If Mictlan ever returns,
               only a descendant of the supreme
               god Huitzilopochtli, a warrior
               armed with Huitzu's serpent sword,
               can vanquish him. But if he fails,
               and Mictlan consumes his heart, the
               darkness will devour this world.
                    (beat, brighter)
               Thank you so much for visiting!

The little crowd starts to disperse. Ms. Romero walks toward
the door, with Monique and Martin in a tow. Both whine:

          MONIQUE   MARTIN
     I'm bored!   Me too!

                    MS. ROMERO
               We're leaving soon, have a little
               patience!

                    XANA/MICTLAN (O.S.)
               Aren't you two adorable!?

Ms Romero turns to see smiling Xana/Mictlan, who pinches
Monique's cheek.

                    XANA/MICTLAN (CONT'D)
               Look at those plump little tykes.
                    (to Ms. Romero)
               You're the chaperone of those young
               people from New Mexico? Can I speak
               to you?

                    MS. ROMERO
               Oh no, what did my kids do now?

> XANA/MICTLAN
> It's nothing like that...

> MS. ROMERO
> (sees Rafa)
> Rafa! Could you please watch your
> brother and sister for a moment?

Rafa GROANS in displeasure, but takes Monique and Martin's hands. Ms. Romero walks out of the room with Xana/Mictlan.

ANGLE ON: at the other end of the room, Safi browses artifacts. She hears INDISTINCT WHISPERS, in Nahuatl language, and notices a strange sight:

A HUMMINGBIRD flitting about indoors, circling the displays.

Safi glances: nobody pays the hummingbird any attention. It flies out of the room -- and Safi follows.

INT. MUSEUM - CONTINUOUS

Alejandro/Xolotl walks toward the exit, but slows down sensing something. He SNIFFS like a dog, narrows his eyes.

ALEJANDRO POV: in X-RAY vision once more, A WISP OF GOLDEN PARTICLES in the air, tinkling towards his nose.

He follows the 'smell' to the entrance to the Room 1 from where it's spreading. He peers inside to find --

The visiting crowd basking in a transparent golden haze.

INT. ROOM 1 - CONTINUOUS

Alejandro/Xolotl approaches Kiki.

> ALEJANDRO/XOLOTL
> I smell Huitzu!

> KIKI
> I thought, I was mistaken. But my
> nose is not as good as yours,
> *Xolotl*.

> ALEJANDRO/XOLOTL
> Nobody's is, Coqui.
> (points with his eyes)
> Those kids --

> KIKI/COQUI
> A soccer team from New Mexico!

They both stare at Calian LAUGHING with Rafa and Anaya.

                    ALEJANDRO/XOLOTL
          The tall boy... So strong and
          beautiful. The kind that walked up
          the steps to be slaughtered.
                    (beat, thoughtfully)
          You know, the last of the Aztec
          royalty had escaped to the South
          West and lived with the Acoma
          tribe...

                    KIKI
          He must be the descendant! The heir
          of Huitzu! Their chaperone said
          they're leaving tonight...

                    ALEJANDRO/XOLOTL
          Good. The sooner, the better.

                    KIKI
          I must warn Xonaxi!

Kiki hurries out.

INT. ROOM 2 - DAY

Smaller, darker, and deserted. The WHISPERS seem louder here.
The HUMMINGBIRD LANDS ON THE SHOULDER of --

An oversized STATUE of Huitzilopochtli, looking just as in
Safi's childhood dream, its eyes closed.

Safi stops and stares at it, completely entranced. Gradually,
she begins to hear something...

A HEARTBEAT. Slowly, she moves close, unable to look away:

The 'statue's' chest moves as if a heart is indeed beating
within it. She stretches her hand to touch it --

SAFI'S VISION: The 'statue's' EYES snap open and, just like
in her old dream, their multiple irises peer deep into the
depths of her soul.

He leans forward and places a small, glowing, bejeweled
object in Safi's outstretched hand as we --

                                        ENTER MONTAGE:

-- In the dimness, a handful of spectral Tzitzimimeh put
directional arrows along the passages.

-- Blood is sprayed on the exhibits, the Halloween and the
Day-of-the-dead decorations.

-- Some of the latter shudder, briefly animating as some strange life enters them, then returning to lifeless form for the moment.

                              BACK TO:

Lying on the floor, Safi GASPS, opens her eyes and sits up. She opens her palm and gapes at --

A BEAUTIFUL AZTEC NECKLACE, a talisman/pendant of gold and jade in a form of a curled feathered serpent-dragon.

She looks around to find that the light and the oversized statue are gone. In their place is only a replica of the stylized Huitzilopochtli plaque, depicting him, per the tradition, with a HUMMINGBIRD.

INT. ROOM 1 - CONTINUOUS

The teens wander about, bored. Rafa, with his brother and sister, Calian, and Anaya among them.

Alejandro circles the loose group surreptitiously, nostrils flaring. He stops, SNIFFS, as if he lost the scent.

Safi walks in, stares around, then glances at the necklace in her palm, torn. She SIGHS, and walks toward Alejandro.

                    SAFI
          I'm sorry... sir? Do you work here?

Alejandro turns to her, startled.

                    ALEJANDRO/XOLOTL
          Can I help you?

                    SAFI
          I found something... in one of the
          rooms.

She opens her palm to show him the necklace. Stunned, Alejandro gapes at her, then at the necklace.

                    ALEJANDRO/XOLOTL
             (shakes his head)
          It is _not_ a display.

                    SAFI
          Whoever dropped it might come
          back...
             (resigned)
          It should go to the lost and found.

She extends her open palm with the necklace to him. Beat, he peers at her. Smiles.

                    ALEJANDRO/XOLOTL
          Finders keepers!

                    SAFI
               (brightens)
          You sure?

                    ALEJANDRO/XOLOTL
               (at the necklace)
          Do you know what it is?

                    SAFI
          I think it's a pendant dedicated to
          the great Huitzilopochtli... It's
          Xiuhcoatl, isn't it?

                    ALEJANDRO/XOLOTL
          Not just a pendant. It's Huitzu's
          talisman: the protector serpent
          sword of the great ruler god.

He seizes her hand holding out the necklace, and suddenly
TIME FREEZES as Alejandro/Xolotl sees --

                    QUICK FLASHES:

-- a BEDROOM in the group home. Safi lies seemingly asleep as
CARL looms over her. He reaches out, attempting to grope her -
- she suddenly reaches under her pillow, withdraw the BREAD
KNIFE from earlier, and STABS him in the stomach.

He SCREAMS, recoils, grabbing his stomach, blood pouring. She
jumps out of bed - and over him as he collapses --

-- Panicking, Safi runs through the dark kitchen with an oil
can in tow, pouring flammable liquid all over the place. She
then turns on the gas stove.

-- She hurriedly runs into the kids' bedroom, waking them up
and ushering them to exit the house. Though confused, they
follow her lead.

-- She searches the drawers in the group home's office, finds
a bundle of cash, grabs it and hurries for the exit.

-- OUTSIDE of the group home, she tosses a lit MATCH onto a
trail of accelerant leading into the house. The entire
structure is set ablaze as the other kids watch, stunned.

-- As the fire rages, she uses a rock to smash the window of
the car parked outside and rushes in. She fumbles starting
the vehicle, clumsily backs into a trash can, reverses, bumps
into another car in front. Then, finally, she speeds away.

                                        BACK TO:

The present, where Alejandro lets go of her hand. Time
'unfreezes' and Safi wakes up with a small GASP. She looks
around, baffled.

                    ALEJANDRO/XOLOTL (CONT'D)
          How long are you staying in town?

                    SAFI
          Oh... I... another day. There's
          still a lot I'd like to see.

                    ALEJANDRO/XOLOTL
               (re: the talisman)
          Don't show that to anyone. There
          might be some suspicious folks
          around for the big event.
               (gazing at her shrewdly)
          Of course, a lot of police too.
          Tonight, they'll be checking IDs,
          searching cars, to see if any are
          stolen. I hope you can afford a
          place to stay. The room prices are
          going to be sky-high tonight. That
          high school soccer team from New
          Mexico are in a hurry to get out of
          Dodge, they won't stay another
          night.

Safi stares at him like a deer in the headlights and scurries
off toward the exit. He watches her intently, then walks out
of the room through another door.

EXT. MUSEUM'S PARKING LOT - CONTINUOUS

Safi puts the necklace on as she walks. She admires the
talisman, then hides it under her collar. She stops short,
gaping at:

A GROUP OF SECURITY GUARDS and A COUPLE POLICE OFFICERS
lingering by her car. One of them cups his face, presses it
to the window, peering inside.

Safi quickly turns and hurries back to the building.

                                                  CUT TO:

INT. ROOM 1 - MOMENTS LATER

Safi is in mid-conversation with a puzzled Anaya.

                    ANAYA
          ... So, what, you want to return to
          the states with us?! Are your Arab
          parents marrying you off to some
          old perv?

                    SAFI
               (sighs)
          No. See, I kind of lied. I'm in a
          bit of trouble...

Anaya listens to her, concerned. Suddenly, Ms. Romero's voice
comes over the speaker:

                    MS. ROMERO/MICTLAN (V.O.)
               (cheery)
          Listen up, Acoma Pueblo High School
          soccer team! A change of plans! The
          museum curators have a marvelous
          surprise for us! Follow the arrows
          to lobby two...

INT. CURATOR'S OFFICE - CONTINUOUS

Kiki hurries inside and is surprised to spot Ms.
Romero/Mictlan from behind, just finishing up her speech on
the radio:

                    MS. ROMERO/MICTLAN
          ... For great Halloween fun!

                    KIKI
          Excuse me! What are you doing?!

Kiki GASPS, now noticing the broken container in the
terrarium --

Just as Ms Romero/Mictlan turns to them with black eyes,
blowing green smoke right into Kiki's face.

Kiki's eyes now go all-black for a moment as Mictlan takes
possession. Ms. Romero wakes up.

                    MS. ROMERO
          How on Earth did I get here?!
               (at the knife in her
                hands)
          Jesus, Mary and Joseph!

                    KIKI/MICTLAN
               (smiling)
          Not quite.

Kiki/Mictlan snatches the bloody knife from her and viciously
SLASHES her chest wide open.

INT. SERVICE CORRIDOR - CONTINUOUS

Alejandro/Xolotl hurries along the dimly lit corridor, then
makes a turn as he passes a HVAC area and stops abruptly,
spotting something. He does a double take, stricken --

Some distance ahead, a SPECTRAL crouching TZITZIMIMEH
scurries on all-fours. It pauses, staring back at him, then
hurries on with a CHITTERING SOUND.

He watches it disappear in the dark.

                    KIKI/MICTLAN (O.S.) (CONT'D)
          Xolotl!

Alejandro/Xolotl turns to him/her as he/she approaches.
Alejandro/Xolotl's nostrils tremble like a dog's as he
SNIFFS. He looks down at the bloody knife in Kiki's hands.

                    KIKI/MICTLAN (CONT'D)
          Don't worry, I'm not interested in
          your worn body. Plus, I need an
          assistant. Wouldn't it be nice to
          work together again, like old
          times?

Alejandro/Xolotl looks over to find the TZITZIMIMEHS dragging
past them the pale corpses of Ms. Romero and Enrique.

                    KIKI/MICTLAN (CONT'D)
              (at the Tzitzimimehs)
          Sweet darlings. Loyal to a fault.
          Sniffed me out as soon as I was
          free, and showed up like good
          soldiers. But they're not the
          brightest lot.

                    ALEJANDRO/XOLOTL
          Why do you need my help? You seem
          able-bodied enough.

                    KIKI/MICTLAN
          Funny story. I consumed one
          goddess' heart and reside in the
          body of another. Which gives me
          just enough magic to _start_ my
          quest. But. I need so many more
          hearts, Xolotl! Strong, young
          hearts. And one heart in
          particular, that will make me just
          as strong as Huitzu once was! I
          know you smelled it too -- the
          blood of your dear old boss. And
          you probably already know, his
          descendant is here, on these very
          premises.

                    ALEJANDRO/XOLOTL
              (shrugs)
          Huitzu was my boss eons ago. I
          could care less about human scum.
          Happy hunting.

He turns to walk away.

                    KIKI/MICTLAN
Not all human scum, surely? You
cared so much about one particular
human, you gave up your immortality
for her.

Alejandro/Xolotl sags and turns back.

                    KIKI/MICTLAN (CONT'D)
Oh, yes, just as we speak --

He looks up alongside Alejandro/Xolotl:

The ceiling has disappeared, and in the black sky above, the
stars shimmer.

ALEJANDRO/XOLOTL'S POV: some of the clusters are, in fact,
the Tzitzimimehs flying across in a single formation.

                    KIKI/MICTLAN (CONT'D)
My winged troops are en route to
your home. You know how fast they
can travel through airspace!
    (beat)
I'm sure your lovely wife would
prefer to join you before the world
ends. You two can live out the rest
of your lives somewhere peaceful...
away from all the carnage. That's
what you always were after, was it
not?
    (beat)
They won't harm her, unless you
don't cooperate of course.

Alejandro/Xolotl processes this grimly.

                    ALEJANDRO/XOLOTL
    (beat, grave)
If I'm involved in this, things
must be done properly --

                    KIKI/MICTLAN
I agree. The tributes must be
sacrificed according to tradition,
not wasted!

                    ALEJANDRO/XOLOTL
There'll be no cheating, no
shortcuts!

                    KIKI/MICTLAN
I've always admired your attention
to detail. Welcome aboard!

INT. LOBBY 2 - CONTINUOUS

The lights are dim. The teens trickle in, including Rafa with
Monique and Martin. Anaya and Safi enter last. Kiki/Mictlan
faces them, all smiles.

                    KIKI/MICTLAN (CONT'D)
          Niltse, piltin! You've met me
          already. I'm Miss Kiki, and I'm in
          charge in this fine establishment!

Kiki/Mictlan adapts an exaggerated, turned-to-eleven persona,
very unlike their earlier self. He stands at the center of
the room, smiling coquettishly at the arrivals.

Alejandro/Xolotl is here too, his face more haggard than
ever. His eyes meet Safi's, widen in unpleasant surprise. He
holds her gaze for a few moments, then looks away.

                    RAFA
          Hey, where's mom... Ms. Romero?

                    KIKI/MICTLAN
          Oh, we gave her a gift card and
          sent her to the museum's coffee
          shop. She deserves a nice break
          too, don't you think?

                    RAFA
             (at Monique and Martin)
          So I'm stuck with them?!

                    KIKI/MICTLAN
             (to Alejandro/Xolotl)
          We don't mind the little rug-rats,
          do we? Not at all!
             (back to Rafa)
          All of you kids are going to have
          an absolute *blast!*

Kiki/Mictlan GIGGLES for no apparent reason.

                    SAFI
             (sotto, to Anaya)
          That... Kiki... seems, like,
          weirder.

                    RAFA
             (to Kiki/Mictlan)
          What kinda fun are we talking?

                    KIKI/MICTLAN
          Today, you, my handsome lads, will
          have a chance to show how worthy
          you are of your brave ancestors!
             (MORE)

                    KIKI/MICTLAN (CONT'D)
          Whoever outplays the house, will
          receive a warrior's honor!

Surprised but excited MURMURS among the teens.

                    CALIAN
               (eager)
          How do we 'outplay the house?'

                    KIKI/MICTLAN
          You must get through this --
               (theatrically)
          -- Glorious, ghastly, gasp-inducing
          maze of horrors! But I warn you,
          not everyone will make it.

                    RAFA
               (scoffs)
          What have you got in there... death
          traps?

The guys LAUGH.

                    KIKI/MICTLAN
          Oh, just some cute little trials we
          set up for you... You may be
          detained -- er, prevented from
          finishing the game and getting your
          reward. And no flash photography or
          outside calls while you're here. We
          have some delicate electronic
          equipment!
               (chuckles)
          Just kiddin'! There's no reason for
          you to relinquish your precious
          devices. They won't work here
          anyway!

Safi doesn't have one, but a few teens take their phones out
and try to use them. They GROAN collectively.

                    TEENS
          Hey, mine's dead completely!/Mine
          too!/This sucks!

                    CALIAN
               (to Kiki/Mictlan, at his
                dead phone)
          You can do that?! I mean, if we
          just didn't have a connection I get
          it, but to drain the power --

                    ALEJANDRO/XOLOTL
               (sotto, to Kiki/Mictlan)
          You went overboard with this!

                    CALIAN
               (impressed)
          ... I mean, this is straight up
          trippy!

Kiki/Mictlan smiles, gives Alejandro a "told you so" look.

                    RAFA
               (to Kiki/Mictlan)
          Okay, uh, miss, if we *get* through
          the --
               (mocks)
          'Maze of horrors' or whatever, what
          kinda reward are we talking about?!
          Show me the money, honey!

                    KIKI/MICTLAN
               (glares)
          I see not everybody here has a
          fighting spirit!

                    CALIAN
          Oh, we do, Sir... I mean, Ma'am, we
          definitely do! The scarier the
          better. Let's get it!

The boys LAUGH, HOOT, etc. Kiki/Mictlan smiles at Calian.

                    KIKI/MICTLAN
          Spoken like a true leader!
               (at Anaya)
          And you be Anaya Romero herself.
          Your school's most talented and
          beautiful cheerleader?!

Anaya curtsies, pleased, smiling.

                    KIKI/MICTLAN (CONT'D)
          Ms. Romero told me you intend to
          become a dancer? Are you just as
          talented as you are pretty, my
          dear?

Anaya PURRS in confirmation.

                    KIKI/MICTLAN (CONT'D)
          How exciting! Then we shall have a
          dance-off for you! And we'll record
          it... my assistant here --
               (re: Alejandro/Xolotl)
          Is a professional cameraman. And if
          you're as good as they say, I'll
          send the video to a man I know in
          Los Angeles! He scouts dancers for
          music videos!

Anaya jumps up and down, SQUEALS in delight. Safi notices
that Rafa makes a face, and can't help smirking herself.

                    KIKI/MICTLAN (CONT'D)
          Good luck to you all!

He/she walks off with Alejandro/Xolotl, excited. Out of the
group's earshot:

                    KIKI/MICTLAN (CONT'D)
          The Huitzu's scent is strong!

                    ALEJANDRO/XOLOTL
          I'll make sure the boy is disposed
          of last. What of the Assyrian girl?
          She shouldn't be here at all. I
          could get rid of her...

                    KIKI/MICTLAN
          Too much trouble. Plus, to
          discriminate her because of her
          origins would be against the spirit
          of the era, don't you think?
               (beat)
          Let her be _honored_ with the rest.

                    JANITOR/XOLOTL
          How progressive of you. And when
          should we... _honor_ her?

                    KIKI/MICTLAN
               (playfully)
          Whenever the urge strikes us.

Behind them, in the lobby, the lights dim, and the large
doors leading into the depth of the museum open by themselves
invitingly.

The teens walk through, GIGGLING, goofing off, acting rowdy,
as always as they check out the HALLOWEEN EXHIBITS
REPERTOIRE, all affixed with Aztec motifs.

Walking behind, Safi watches as Little Monique and Martin
keeps close to their brother. Rafa squeezes their hands
reassuringly, murmurs something to them.

Safi notices a STRANGE SHIMMERING within the exhibit's dark
recesses...

                    RAFA
          Well, so far, it's pretty lame...

Safi hears some quiet CHITTERING. She squints, clocking:

SCATTERED SPARKS/MOVEMENT in the deep shadows in the
periphery, swirling around the teens.

Safi hurries to catch up to Anaya:

                    SAFI
              (points)
         Did you see... like sparks or
         something over there?

Anaya glances, makes a face.

                    ANAYA
         Some special effect probably.

Wandering alone ahead, Donald notices the same EVIL CLOWN
EXHIBIT Eric used to scare him earlier. He glances back,
checks that the approaching teens don't see him, and hides
behind the clown.

He threads his arms into the clown's sleeves, grins,
anticipating his pay-back.

                    DONALD
         Oh, I'm gonna get you fuckers *good*.

As he peeks from behind the dummy, we see --

THE CLOWN'S HEAD rotate beside him, eyes staring at Donald's
profile -- Sensing movement, Donald turns around and meets
the clown's garish face seconds before it --

COMES ALIVE, eyes glowing and maw opening to reveal a row of
jagged FANGS as it transforms into an AZTEC DEMON!

                    DONALD (CONT'D)
         Holy shit!

The clown POUNCES, sinking its teeth into Donald's face as --

ANGLE ON: the other teens look up upon hearing a terrified,
choked SQUEAL which is abruptly cut short.

                    ERIC
              (laughing, calls out)
         Nice try, Donny boy!

As they continue to walk in that direction, they see the
clown - as just another inert display again. There's no sign
of Donald.

                    RAFA
              (calls)
         Hey, Donny?! Where'd you go?

                    ERIC
         You can come out now, douchebag!

Calian shrugs.

                    CALIAN
          If he wants to play hide-and-seek,
          that's his business. Let's get us
          some *chedda'*!

The teens CHEER, except Safi (who winces not understanding
the slang word), and continue on.

INT. GAME AREA - CONTINUOUS

Suddenly, an eerie DRUM MUSIC COMES ON. A LARGE, GREY RUBBER
BALL flies out of nowhere, grazing and knocking down BLY.

                    BLY
              (laughing, groaning)
          Ouch! Man, that hurt!

The ball disappears for a moment, then reappears again,
WHOOSHING past Calian. He dodges it, perking up.

                    SAFI
          It's an Aztec game! That ball is
          solid rubber! Don't try to catch
          it, it'll break your fingers!

Calian dodges the ball fairly easily again.

                    CALIAN
          Dope!
              (eager, to Safi)
          What're we supposed to do?

                    RAFA
              (mocking)
          Yeah, tell us, oh wise professor!

Safi glances around and above them spots --

A stone hoop, seemingly floating unattached in the darkness
above...

                    SAFI
          You have to send it through that
          loop! Use your backs, hips, and
          butts!

The ball flies at her. She SQUEAKS and deftly bops it with
her shoulder and back, surprising herself.

                    CALIAN
              (to Safi)
          Damn! You got game! Stay close,
          okay?

Safi beams. The ball reappears. The boys dash, grappling to
push each other into the passage of the ball as they LAUGH.

Rafa is preoccupied with keeping his brother and sister out of harm's way. Safi clocks this.

                    MONIQUE
          We want to play too!

                    RAFA
          No way! It could hurt you!

He leads them (complaining a bit) to a corner between the divider panels, and they crouch there.

Anaya SQUEALS as the ball flies too close to her. Rafa ducks down further.

                    RAFA (CONT'D)
              (to the kids)
          Stay low, and don't stick out!

Following Safi's example while being pursued by the appearing and disappearing ball, the teens hit it with their hips. They GRUNT as it smacks against them, then giggle.

As it flies at her, Safi attempts to kick it up toward the hoop -- only to watch in frustration as the ball _resists going where it was sent_, disappearing in the dark instead.

                    SCOTTY
          What the hell!?

Spread out by now, they all gawk around looking for the ball. A beat. Then, suddenly --

It comes SOARING in from the opposite direction, headed straight for Scotty! He tries to outrun it, swerving along the passage between the divider walls. But it appears to follow him.

                    SCOTTY (CONT'D)
              (running from the ball)
          Hey, why me?! Get off, you stupid --

The ball hits him in the back _HARD_, propelling him _out of everyone's sight_ and --

Into A VISCOUS WALL COVERED IN SCALY SKIN. It SPROUTS REPTILIAN EYES that open and stare at him --

He SQUEAKS in terror and desperately tries to scoot off backwards on his butt, only for --

SUCTION-CUPPED, SLIME COATED TENTACLES to stretch out and entwine him. He tries to tear away in panic.

                    SCOTTY (CONT'D)
          Oh my God! No! Let me go!

                                        BACK TO:

The TEENS, now on edge. The reappeared ball zeroes on Bly,
who tries to outrun it.

Amidst the chaos, the ball chases him _out of everybody's_
sight, and HITS him square in the chest, sending him into yet
another wall, covered with green goo.

Bly sticks to it like a fly on flypaper.

                    BLY
               (still laughing)
          Yo! This shit is crazy!

Then, with a GULP, the wall starts to suck him into its
surface. He GIGGLES at first, then becomes frightened as the
wall absorbs him further.

                    BLY (CONT'D)
          Hold up! Guys?!..
               (at the wall)
          Hey, stop it!..

But green GOO fills his mouth before he can shout further,
silencing his cries as he --

COMPLETELY DISAPPEARS within the goopy wall.

BACK WITH THE OTHERS. The ball reappears and flies past
Calian. He tries to kick it, but misses. The ball heads
instead for --

Antonio, who tries in vain to get out of its way.

                    ANTONIO
          Why the fuck is it following me?!

                    CALIAN
          It doesn't follow anybody, dumbass!
          Get out of its way!

Safi watches, puzzled, realizing that --

It _does look_ like the ball is _targeting_ Antonio, who trips
and falls, sliding on his belly --

Behind another display and _out of his friends' sight_.

As the ball flies just above him, Antonio watches it.

                    ANTONIO
                  (sotto)
          That's right, ball-bitch.

He then feels something, looks down at --

A GIANT eyeless SLUG swallowing his feet like a python!

He kicks at it, trying to free himself as it sucks him in
deeper, up to his hips.

                    ANTONIO (CONT'D)
          Holy mother of fuck!

He continues to struggle, but the slug doesn't relent.

                    ANTONIO (CONT'D)
          Let me go! Get off me!

He manages to wiggle out, slides along the floor, covered by
slime. He attempts to stand, only to slip due to the
gelatinous material.

                    ANTONIO (CONT'D)
                  (calls)
          Dudes!.. Help!..

He look up, to find himself staring directly into a GIANT
OPEN MAW at the other end of the slug, also eyeless, but
armed with double rows of sharp teeth. He SCREAMS as the
creature STRIKES down --

BACK WITH THE OTHERS. They hear HIS SCREAM CUT SHORT.

                    RAFA
          Hey, what was that!? Did you guys --

Before Rafa can continue, he too is chased by the ball. With
great effort, he manages to dodge it successfully. He glances
off, and sees --

Antonio's feet disappearing from view as he is limply dragged
away between some divider walls.

Rafa furrows his brow, but the ball flies by again, forcing
him to jump and roll out of its way.

ON MONIQUE AND MARTIN: Monique hears an odd CHITTERING.

                    MONIQUE
          Do you hear that?

                    MARTIN
          Hear what?

Monique now notices the same 'SHIMMERING' that Safi noticed
before. Intrigued, she gets up and follows it.

                    MARTIN (CONT'D)
          Where you goin'!?

He gets up and hurries after her.

INT. ANOTHER AREA - CONTINUOUS

Monique continues to follow the CHITTERING and shimmering,
Martin on her heels.

                    MARTIN (CONT'D)
          Slow down, would you!

                    MONIQUE
               (points)
          Do you see her?!

                    MARTIN
          See who?!

                    MONIQUE
          The shiny lady!

Martin gapes, puzzled.

                    MARTIN
               (whines)
          Where?! I don't see anything!

MONIQUE's POV: she spots a skeletal TZITZIMIMEH, scurrying
somewhere, disappearing out of the view.

She hurries, Martin running after her, as they enter --

INT. CAVE-LIKE AREA - CONTINUOUS

Monique enters first and sees:

MORE SHIMMERING TZITZIMIMEHS, like insects feeding their
queen bee as they surround Kiki/Mictlan, crouching over --

BLY, lying dead on the floor with his chest flayed open. They
ghoulishly dine on his HEART!

Monique's jaw drops, frozen in sheer terror. Martin catches
up with her. As soon as he sees the awful scene, he goes to
scream, but Monique clamps her hand over his mouth. She
quickly shuttles him away as --

Kiki/Mictlan turns, sensing a presence.

INT. GAME AREA - CONTINUOUS

The ball FLIES past us once again, aimed this time at Rafa.
Just as it's about to make impact with his head --

Safi pulls him out of the way.

                    SAFI
               (screams to Calian)
          This is way too dangerous!

Rafa sees the ball coming, jumps and nails it with two closed
fists, sending it toward the loop. He WINCES in pain as the
loop floats off, avoiding the ball.

                    RAFA
          That's bullshit! This game is
          rigged!

Calian, like an action-hero, jumps agilely up and hits the
ball with his shoulder.

                    CALIAN
               (screams)
          Nah, it's just hard! I bet I can
          make the goal, though!

Safi steps onward, trying to avoid the ball. She ultimately
finds herself in a narrow space between two exhibits, alone
for a beat.

Then, she hears a SWISHING sound. She whips around and her
eyes widen --

Seeing the ball headed at her like a speeding bullet, about
to crack her skull, when, at the last minute, it suddenly
flies directly up, missing her dome.

Her eyes catch a movement at the end of the passage --

And a dark, semi-canine silhouette gesturing as if he were
directing the ball's flight.

                    SAFI
               (to the silhouette)
          Hey!

But the figure steps off, dissolving in the dark. She hears,
at some distance, behind:

                    RAFA (O.S.)
               (calls)
          Monique?! Martin?!

Safi turns and hurries back, and out into the open. She spots
Rafa running the same area, looking around.

                    RAFA (CONT'D)
               (to the rest)
          Hey! Where did the kids go?!

Safi catches up, joins the search.

                    RAFA (CONT'D)
               (calls)
          Hey, everybody!

They try to gather up the group, but the flying ball keeps
breaking them apart, almost as if on purpose.

It flies in between Chad and Calian. They CHEER as Eric kicks
the ball toward the loop, but he too misses.

As the ball flies through again, Rafa SWEARS and drops to the
ground to avoid being hit. Safi YELPS as she deflects the
ball with her backpack.

The ball reappears and flies straight at Calian, who kicks it
awkwardly toward the loop --

ENTER SLOW MO: as the ball swerves and *flies gracefully*
through the loop, even though it should have missed it going
by the laws of physics.

                    CALIAN
               (roars)
          Fuck yeah! I'm king of the world,
          baby!

                    RAFA
          Weird...

                    CALIAN
          Weird?! You guys just suck at this!

Out of the blue, the ball comes HURTLING in again, headed
straight for Rafa -- Safi jumps into the ball's path, and
manages to hit it with the backpack -- but only slightly
deflects it off the course while Rafa backs off, startled --

-- only to trip and fall, while the ball smashes into a wall
a few feet from Rafa, and gets stuck.

Rafa crawls to it to take a closer look, gapes:

The ball is not smooth like before, but is instead covered in
glistening, razor sharp obsidian blades! One blade is reamed
into the wall, suspending it.

He tries to pull the ball out but everything seems to melt
into amorphous goo as he touches it. The slime runs through
his fingers. He shakes his hands furiously.

                        RAFA
            Yuck!

He rubs his hands off on his jeans, gets up and hurries
toward the others.

                        RAFA (CONT'D)
            I think that crazy MOFO's trying to
            murder us for real! I need to find
            my brother and sister!

                        ERIC
            Chill! They're here somewhere...
            just wandered off, man.

                        SAFI
            I'll look with you!

                        MONIQUE (O.S.)
                (screams)
            He ate Bly! He ate Bly!

They see Monique and Martin running in. The MUSIC stops. Out
of breath, the kids talk hurriedly, interrupting each other.

          MARTIN   MONIQUE (CONT'D)
Bly was on the floor! He was   Miss Kiki... she... he was
all cut up!   eating Bly's insides!

                        ERIC
                (to Monique)
            Didn't your mom teach you not to
            lie?! Oh, at least, lie better?

                        RAFA
                (to Eric, sternly)
            My sister doesn't lie!
                (beat)
            But she _can_ get confused --

                        MONIQUE
            No! We saw him! He was eating Bly's
            guts! I'm telling you!

                        RAFA
            Where?! Show us!

Rafa, Safi, Calian, Anaya, Eric, and Chad hurry to follow the
kids. Monique pulls Rafa's hand, brave now. Safi clocks this.

INT. CAVE-LIKE AREA - CONTINUOUS

They enter, look around: All is quiet, deserted.

                    MONIQUE
                (points)
          It was right there, on the floor!

They check the floor. Chad's eyes widen.

                    CHAD
          Hey, it's blood! It's blood!

They crowd around a large pool of blood on the floor. A few
of them, including Anaya, follows the splatter --

She SQUEALS, spotting: a skinned torso hanging from a rack! A
beat, then --

                    RAFA (O.S.)
                (cooling off)
          It's a fake, guys!

Anaya turns to see Rafa dipper a finger in the 'blood.' He
rubs it, smells. Then licks it.

                    RAFA (CONT'D)
          Strawberry syrup.

                    ERIC
                (chuckling)
          Told ya. These kids are little
          liars!

                    MONIQUE
                (almost crying)
          But I *did* see it! Honest!

                    CHAD
          Yeah, right. Maybe y'all should be
          child actors.

                    RAFA
          If my sister says she saw
          something, she did!

                    ANAYA
                (to Monique and Martin)
          It's all make-believe, guys!
          They're just trying to scare us!

                    MONIQUE
          It looked real! And there were
          these... these shiny ladies,
          sitting all around!

                    SAFI
                (to Monique, alert)
          What do you mean, 'shiny ladies?'

MONIQUE
They were bony! And... like...

SAFI
Sparkly?

Monique nods.

MARTIN
I didn't see any bony sparkly
ladies!

ERIC
(to Safi, at Monique)
You're putting this bullshit into
the kid's head now?!

SAFI
(to Anaya)
Didn't you see them too? Like
little sparks moving?

Anaya shrugs.

SAFI (CONT'D)
They must be Tzitzimimehs! Remember
that slide during the
presentation?! They're these demons
that only women can see!

CALIAN
Damn. I wonder what kinda tech
these guys are using. I mean, to
kill all our phones like that?!

SAFI
But if it's tech, how could they
make something that only girls can
see -- and the boys won't?!

CHAD
(patronizing)
See, in the states, we have more
advanced computer effects than
you've ever seen in your country!

SAFI
No way. It's not possible.

RAFA
Tech or not, they should've told us
not to bring little kids into this
hellhole. They could get PTSD from
this shit! If my mom knew, she
would never have let them come!

                    CALIAN
          They probably just aren't that
          uptight about the kids getting
          scared in Mexico.

                    CHAD
          Totally! That makes this place even
          more lit!

                    RAFA
          The ball that flew at me was
          covered in blades! And then it...
          just melted!

                    SAFI
          Blades? As in, like, knife blades?

                    RAFA
          Yes, as in deadly fricking blades!
          It nearly killed me!

                    CHAD
          You're so full of shit you stink up
          the place.

Rafa smacks him, Chad smacks him back, a mini-tussle
commences, with angry Rafa coming out on top.

                    CALIAN
          Chill, dudes!

Rafa and Chad break off, Chad LAUGHING.

                    RAFA
          Where is everybody? I mean, where
          did Bly get off to anyway?
               (calls)
          Donny?! Bly?!

                    ANAYA
               (calls)
          Scotty?! Antonio?!

The teens wanders around a bit too, calling out for their
friends.

                    CALIAN
          Miss Kiki specifically warned us
          that the losers would be detained!

                    RAFA
          What kinda lame-ass game is this?!
          We barely got in, and it's all over
          for four of us already!?

                    CALIAN
          They just couldn't hack it, bruh.

                    RAFA
               (mocks)
          And _you_ can?! You just want to win!
          It's all you think about. I think
          your --
               (mocking)
          Miss Kiki --
               (normal voice)
          Would bend over for you as a
          reward. That she-man was basically
          drooling when he talked to you!
               (to all)
          Our guys _aren't_ losers! They're the
          best players our school ever had!
          If this _is_ a game, nobody explained
          the rules! They didn't have a
          chance!

                    ERIC
               (to Rafa)
          You're always the one getting into
          trouble! Why are you making such a
          big deal out of this, dude?!

                    RAFA
          I don't like this set up, okay?!
          Something feels... off.

                    CHAD
               (scoffs)
          Whatever.

Rafa's and Safi's eyes meet. He scowls and looks away. She
does the same, visibly stung.

INT. SPACIOUS THROUGHWAY - CONTINUOUS

They exit into an open area with more exhibits: fake dead
gangsters, lying as if shot in a gunfight along a 'country
road' littered with bones, fake cactuses, and tumbleweeds.

Alongside them sits an OLD FORD -- a replica of the Bonny and
Clyde death car, complete with bullet holes, and dummy
skeletons of 'Bony and Clyde.'

Monique and Martin stay close to Rafa, eyeing the car warily.

                    RAFA
               (to Monique and Martin)
          It's nothing. Just fakes. And
          whiteys too! Not even Aztecs! I got
          enough of those.
               (to a dummy, mocking)
                    (MORE)

                    RAFA (CONT'D)
You're not looking too good, dum-
dum.
          (to the rest)
If y'all are so into this stupid
place, fine, I can play along.
          (yelling out)
You hear that, Miss Kiki?! Do your
worst, as long as you don't try to
scare my bro and sis!
          (to Monique and Martin)
Stay close, don't get lost, and
don't freak out, okay?! Nothing you
see here is real!

                    MONIQUE
I'll try. But no promises!

                    ANAYA
          (to the others)
It's so quiet now...

There's MUSIC AGAIN, gradually GROWING IN VOLUME -- an odd
mix of Native Folk and Classic Rock. The surroundings grow
dark, but some light sifts through from the same direction.

Calian grins to them, shrugs, and marches toward it. The rest
follow suit, Monique holds Rafa's hand, Martin holds Safi's.

INT. HALL OF SKELETONS - CONTINUOUS

A large, ominous space. Its ceilings and walls are shrouded
in darkness, lit only at the center with a few torches.

The centerpiece is a flat-topped step-pyramid representing an
Aztec temple, with a small 'landing' on each step, a stage at
the top, and four skeletons positioned around its base.

REVEAL: The music is played by A GROUP OF BLOATED, BLIND
AZTEC DEMON MUSICIAN ANIMATRONICS in monstrous masks, a few
yards from the stage.

Everybody glances expectantly at Safi.

                    SAFI
          (re: the giant skeletons)
Those right there must be
representing the Quinametzin! The
first people that were ever
created... These four giants
supported the Sky in the Rain
world!

                    RAFA
          (sarcastic)
Cool story.

The skeletons suddenly start to jerk/dance WITH THE RISING
MUSIC, slowly at first, then increasing the pace

                    RAFA (CONT'D)
          Great... They're animated too!

The teens notice and stare at --

A FIGURE at the top. First, it stands still as a statue, its
back to the group.

But as the dance starts in earnest, turning and dancing
sinuously to --

REVEAL: it's Kiki/Mictlan dressed as Chalchiuhtlicue, the
goddess of water, in a yellow headdress and a garish skirt.

He beckons Anaya, who stares about awkwardly for a beat.

                    KIKI/MICTLAN
          Come on, girl, it's time for your
          close up!

Growing enthusiastic, Anaya climbs the steps of the pyramid
temple.

Monique and Martin try to hide from Kiki's sight behind Rafa,
who watches Kiki warily.

                    ANAYA
          (excited, to Kiki/Mictlan)
          Where's the camera?!

Kiki/Mictlan gestures across the way at a platform above the
orchestra, where Alejandro/Xolotl, in his priestly regalia
now, stands pointing an old BETAMAX TV CAMERA at the stage.

Anaya beams and starts to dance, imitating the skeletons --

THE BOYS' POV: items of clothing, all the colored like
Chalchiuhtlicue, float down from the ether, dropping onto and
wrapping around Anaya.

Safi squints at a strange shimmering in the air above Anaya.
She focuses and detects a gleaming skeletal figure, then
another, faintly buzzing above Anaya like bees, dressing her.

                    SAFI
          (points, excited)
          Those _are_ the Tzitzimimehs! One...
          two... six of them!

The rest just stare at her, except for Monique, who watches
the Tzitzimimehs:

                    SAFI (CONT'D)
          Do you see them, Monique?!

                    MONIQUE
          The shiny ladies?
               (pulls Rafa's hand)
          Those are the ones I told you
          about!

Rafa squints in the same direction, puzzled.

                    SAFI
               (to Rafa, agitated)
          See!? You don't see them! But your
          sister and I both do! The
          Tzitzimimehs! Guys can't see them.
          It's almost like they're --

                    RAFA
               (to Safi, irritated)
          What?!

                    SAFI
          Magic! *Real* magic!

THEIR POV: The skeletons glow and _grow in size_. Anaya's
dancing becomes wilder and wilder, as if under a spell.

                    CHAD
               (laughing)
          Hey! Calm down, girl!

The rest of the group, except Safi, Rafa, Monique and Martin,
CLAPS, and LAUGHS.

                    SAFI
          They dressed her like goddess
          Chalchiuhtlicue... That's how they
          dressed girls they chose for
          sacrifice!

                    ERIC
               (elbows Rafa)
          I could suggest one more!

                    CALIAN
          Anaya! Careful! Don't fall! Better
          get down! Hey!

The lights dim, and the whole scene, ALONG WITH THE MUSIC,
becomes more sinister. Safi looks up and behind to find that
Alejandro/Xolotl has disappeared.

                    SAFI
               (screams to Anaya)
          There's no camera! Something's up!

Anaya pays no attention, continues gyrating maniacally.

                    CALIAN
          We've got to get her down!

He runs toward the stage, but before he can get to Anaya, the
Tzitzimimehs -- invisible to him -- block his path. He
staggers backwards, bewildered.

                    CALIAN (CONT'D)
          What was that?!

He squints, but can't see a thing.

                    SAFI
          That's the Tzitzimimehs! You can't
          see them!

                    CHAD
             (mocks her)
          Oh, yeah! Only loaded, stuck-up
          Arabs can see 'em, right?

Eric LAUGHS.

                    SAFI
          I'm not an Arab! And my name is
          Safi! And for the last time, men
          can't see them!

                    RAFA
             (to Martin and Monique)
          Stay here! Don't wander off, okay?!
             (yells)
          Hey, Anaya! Anaya?!

Anaya's head lolls as if she's been stricken with exhaustion.

                    ERIC
          Fine!

He climbs up the pyramid steps.

SAFI'S POV: The TZITZIMIMEHS bolt forward to intercept him.

                    SAFI
          Watch out! On your right!

RAFA'S POV: an invisible force pushes Eric off from the
right, sending him crashing to the ground:

                    ERIC
             (moan)
          That hurt! Sonofabitch!

He scrambles up, GROANING. Monique and Martin back off behind
the group, watch the proceedings with wide eyes.

                    RAFA
               (yells)
          Let's try together!

They all launch into action.

While the Tzitzimimehs are busy attempting to fend off the
boys' frontal assault, Safi leads the charge to the edge of
the stage, climbing up one step at a time, getting closer and
closer to Anaya when --

A couple of Tzitzimimehs notice and fly over to her. They try
to push her off, finally knocking her down. Rafa watches
this, stunned.

Meanwhile, Calian furiously fights the invisible
Tzitzimimehsp. Safi gets up, sees another Tzitzimimeh dive-
bombing him, screams:

                    SAFI
          Calian, on your left!

Calian ducks to the right, climbs the second step --

                    ERIC
               (falling)
          What the hell is happening right
          now!?

                    RAFA
          Hey, everybody! Listen to her!

Boys rush the pyramid, with Safi screaming directions:

                    SAFI
          Duck! From the right! At the back!

The Tzitzimimehs, realizing that Safi is an obstacle, leave
the boys alone, and concentrate on her.

                    SAFI (CONT'D)
          I'll distract them! Hurry!

RAFA'S POV: Safi dodges and swats at the assailants.

Calian, Eric, Rafa, and Chad manage to make some good
progress, but the Tzitzimimehs notice, and three return --

                    SAFI (CONT'D)
          Watch out! They're coming!

Rafa is thrown to the ground once more. Frustration boiling,
he SCREAMS IN RAGE and charges again. He and Calian strike
blindly at the air all around them.

SAFI's POV: abruptly, the Tzitzimimehs retreat as --

The large skeletons lumber closer while Anaya dances at the
top. They enter the fray by grabbing the boys, pulling them
off the stage and dragging them around by their feet.

One of the skeletons grabs Chad, tosses him loose like a rag-
doll. Chad hits the wall with a THUD and slides down,
unconscious. Kiki/Mictlan continues dancing, unhinged.

Monique turns away from the stage. Terrified, she squats with
Martin, their backs to the raging battle. Then, they spot --

A CUTE LITTLE RABBIT hopping across the floor. Martin goes to
head after it.

                         MONIQUE
               We shouldn't...

The Rabbit stares at them with big doe eyes. Incredibly
adorable.

                         MARTIN
               Come on!

Unable to resist, they both jump up and take off after it.

Meanwhile, the battle rages on. Safi almost reaches the top
of the stage, but --

One of the skeletons sees her, pulls her up by her foot. Safi
kicks to no avail. A dot of light beams into her eyes,
momentarily blinding her. She looks up to spot:

Alejandro/Xolotl, shining it down as he stares at her. He
points at his chest/heart and makes a quick, ripping motion.
His eyes shift to the skeleton --

As it lifts her up into the air, she notices a gleaming
normal-sized PULSATING HEART within its rib cage.

Calian grabs one of the torches, waves it madly in front of
the skeleton, trying to force it to release her.

Given a window, Safi reaches into the skeleton's rib cage,
and rips its heart out. Instantly, it collapses into a
motionless pile of bones, dropping her in a heap.

Gritting her teeth in pain, Safi climbs out of the pile.

                    SAFI
              (screams, to the rest)
          Rip their hearts out!

Just then, one of the remaining skeletons leans down and
grasps Rafa, opening his oversized jaws wide to bite down.

Calian jumps on the skeleton's back. It staggers, trying to
tear Calian off. He deftly reaches inside the rib cage and
rips out the pulsating heart. The skeleton collapses.

Calian looks at the heart in his hand -- it appears real,
squishy and blood-soaked.

                    CALIAN
          Gross!

He drops it, only to be distracted by the sound of GNASHING
TEETH directly above.

He looks up to find a THIRD SKELETON, jaws agape, about to
tear his head clean off.

                    KIKI/MICTLAN (O.S.)
              (barks)
          Ayamo!

To Calian's great relief, the skeleton withdraws. As it tries
to straighten up --

Rafa sticks his arm into its rib cage from the back and rips
its heart out, screaming like a cowboy.

                    RAFA
          Yee-haw!

The skeleton collapses--

INT. MUSEUM - ELSEWHERE - CONTINUOUS

The SOUNDS OF THE MUSIC AND THE FIGHTING are distant muted.
Monique and Martin look for the rabbit.

                    MARTIN
          Where did he go?!

                    MONIQUE
              (stops him)
          Do you hear that?!

They listen, now hearing a TODDLER CRYING somewhere nearby.

                    MONIQUE (CONT'D)
          That's not a bunny...

                         MARTIN
              Look!

They see: A SMALL BABY ARM sticking out of a cracked-open
Aztec tomb exhibit, groping as if a toddler was stuck inside.

                         MARTIN (CONT'D)
              That baby's in trouble!

                         MONIQUE
              We'll help you! Don't be afraid!

Martin tries to pry the coffin's lid, Monique grabs the
little hand. Suddenly, the lid flies open to --

REVEAL: A TOAD-LIKE MONSTER'S BULBOUS EYES AND JAGGED TEETH!

They SCREAM as the baby's turns green and reptilian,
fastening around Monique and yanking her into the coffin.

Another 'hand', at the end of a tentacle, darts after Martin.
Before he can run, it grabs him by his ankle, dragging him
towards the coffin as he SCREAMS.

INT. HALL OF SKELETONS - CONTINUOUS

Rafa, Eric, and Safi work together to take down the last
remaining skeleton by ripping out its heart. Anaya dances
like a marionette, seemingly unaware of anything around her.

SAFI'S POV: a couple of flying Tzitzimimehs pull on Anaya'a
limbs with silver strings, controlling her like a puppet.

                         SAFI
                   (screams to the rest)
              She's trapped!

ANGLE ON: above, Kiki/Mictlan steps backwards from the
illuminated stage's edge, melting into the darkness.

Calian climbs vigorously, and nearly reaches the upper stage
when --

A massive BRONZE AXE swings through the space, flying just
past Calian's face like a giant pendulum. Time slows to a
crawl as the blade whirls towards --

ANAYA, viciously DECAPITATING HER in one fell slice. Her head
bounces down the step-pyramid as blood GEYSERS forth from her
neck-stump.

Calian SCREAMS and nearly falls off the stage as it rolls
past him, while her body collapses limply.

Simultaneously, the musicians' bodies 'deflate' like
balloons, releasing GREEN SMOKE that envelops everything.

Caught in the noxious fog, the teens COUGH. The MUSIC QUIETS
DOWN. Everyone shrieks in panic and terror.

The smoke/fog clears. They look around to find --

No trace of the musicians, nor Anaya's body or head.
Unanimated, significantly smaller skeletons are back in their
initial positions.

Rafa looks around, calls out in panic:

                    RAFA (O.S.)
          Monique?! Martin?!

                    ERIC
          Chad? Anyone seen Chad!?

They look for Chad but he's gone. Calian stands up, PANTING.
He clambers onto the top stage, looks around.

                    CALIAN
          There's no blood! It was just a
          trick.

                    ERIC
          Yo, that's sweet! It's like we're
          in a horror movie!

                    SAFI
          Are you blind or something!? Anaya
          is *dead!*

                    CALIAN
          For a second, I almost believed it
          was real too! I thought that
          skeleton was gonna bite my head
          off.
               (laughing)
          But then Miss Kiki screamed
          something, and it stopped!

That gives Safi pause. She stares at the empty platform.

                    ERIC
          I mean, it was gross, but kinda
          cool too, you know. Kiki must've
          got tired of all her squealing, so
          he pulled her out!

Rafa climbs quickly to the top of the flat-topped pyramid-
stage, and screams:

                    RAFA
          Monique! Martin! Get your narrow
          asses over here!
               (MORE)

                    RAFA (CONT'D)
                (at Eric, rolling his
                  eyes)
          I don't give a flying fuck if this
          was a trick, okay! That... she-boy
          is irresponsible AF! And I can't
          even call my mom! Wait until she
          finds out about this!
                (screams)
          Hey, Kiki! We're done here! Show
          your busted face!

As they wait, the lights dim, NASTY WHISPERS AND LAUGHTER
come from all around them. Rafa climbs down.

                    RAFA (CONT'D)
                (to the group)
          Screw this! We have to find the
          kids and get the hell outta here!

Eric GROANS, but Rafa glares at him, shutting him up. The
group follows Rafa out of the skeletons' hall and into --

INT. HAUNTED HOUSE - HALLWAYS - CONTINUOUS

Safi and Eric argue at the back of the reduced group, as
everybody searches around.

                    ERIC
          You ever hear about those stealth
          planes?! It's probably similar
          technology.

                    SAFI
          But how did they make them visible
          only to Monique and me?!

                    ERIC
          Well, you know there might be
          different frequencies of light, and
          maybe, chicks can see in one --

                    SAFI
          That's idiotic.

                    ERIC
                (to Rafa)
          Did she just call me an idiot?

                    RAFA
          What do you expect from her kind?

                    SAFI
                (heated)
          Oh, yeah? And what kind is that?

                    RAFA
          The kind that gets everything
          handed to them on a silver platter.

                    ERIC
               (to all)
          Whatever. Point is, we gotta keep
          playing. Anaya and those dudes are
          just waiting somewhere!
               (to Rafa)
          And I bet your bro and sis are with
          them.

                    RAFA
          After we find the kids, we'll go
          back to that lobby. If the door is
          locked, and we can't find someone
          to let us out, there should be a
          fire alarm we can pull, or an
          intercom, or something.

Eric looks at Calian.

                    CALIAN
          Well... Kiki definitely took this
          way too far. But after we help Rafa
          find the kids... I low-key hope I
          can still finish the game...

                    ERIC
          Same!

Rolled eyes abound. They pass various horror exhibits,
CALLING FOR MONIQUE AND MARTIN. They round a corner and --

A demonic, Aztec-themed 'JACK-IN-A-BOX' jumps out, almost
grabbing Rafa, who SCREAMS and hops away --

The 'Jack-in-a-box' momentarily turns back into an unanimated
exhibit again. Calian and Eric LAUGH at Rafa, who SMACKS
them.

Safi walks alone, arms crossed, miserable.

INT. NOT-SO-FAKE LAKE - CONTINUOUS

They enter an open space meant to duplicate an outdoor scene,
replete with CRICKETS' CHIRPING and FROGS SINGING. There's no
ceiling, but a STARRY SKY instead.

                    ERIC (CONT'D)
               (makes a face)
          Smells like my grandpa's swamp
          cooler.

                         CALIAN
                   Check this out!

They're by a reedy edge of a glistening/reflective lake,
synthetic reeds grown over it, while its further reaches are
shrouded in darkness.

Eric pulls one of the reeds, finding it to be made of
plastic. He pokes the surface with it. It's hard, constructed
with epoxy.

                         ERIC
                   Fakey, fakey, eggs and bakey!

Something seems to move under the semi-clear, glassy surface-
like the scaly back of some prehistoric animal.

                         ERIC (CONT'D)
                   That some Aztec critter again?

                         SAFI
                   I think, it's supposed to be
                   goddess Cipactli. She's a giant
                   toad. Actually, more like a
                   crocodile.

Eric jumps into the 'water.'

                         SAFI (CONT'D)
                   I wouldn't --

Eric doesn't listen, stomps on the hard surface right above
the moving shape. A GIANT SNOUT pokes up beneath him.

                         ERIC
                   Oh man, this is wild!
                        (at the monster)
                   Come and get me, Godzilla!
                        (coos)
                   Who's so big and scary?! Who's a
                   cute monster boy?

                         SAFI
                   It's a girl, actually.

                         ERIC
                   Yeah, duh! Girls are so powerful,
                   they know everything, they see what
                   boys can't see, like those Tzi-Tzi-
                   mamas or whatever --

Eric trails off, noticing Calian's, Rafa's, and Safi's eyes
going moon-shaped.

                         ERIC (CONT'D)
                   What's up?

He turns back to register a monstrous reptiloid HEAD breaking
the surface of the NO LONGER FAKE LAKE. Eric HOLLERS along
with the others as the beast opens its jaws and --

BITES ERIC'S FOOT CLEAN OFF. Blood hoses forth as Eric
SCREAMS in pain. He collapses, splashing into REAL WATER!

Cipactli drags him under in a quick burst of motion. He
disappears into the depths as the lake instantly calms down.

Calian runs to the edge, pokes the surface with the same
stick, but it's fake/hard again! They stare at it, terrified.

                    CALIAN
               (voice shaking)
          It... It bit his foot off! It was
          up close. I saw blood and... and
          bone, and everything! Oh God.
          Eric... *Eric*...
               (beat)
          It can't be real, right?! It can't!

                    SAFI
          Listen!

THE CRICKETS AND FROGS QUIET DOWN. They stare at each other
through the semi-darkness.

                    RAFA
               (calls, desperate)
          Monique! Martin!
               (to Safi)
          You! You know about Aztecs! Figure
          out how to find my brother and
          sister!

Safi gazes around. Above, the stars blink, seeming to move in
one direction. Safi realizes they are not stars -- but the
shimmering Tzitzimimehs!

                    SAFI
          The Tzitzimimehs are on the move!

She hurries in the same direction, Rafa runs right next to
her, Calian following them.

INT. 'PINATAS' HALL' - CONTINUOUS

They hear MUFFLED CRYING, CHANTING, and FOREBODING
MUSIC/DRUMS as they enter. The frog-like, bloated musicians
are here as well, alive once again. The teens halt, startled.

REVERSE: two LARGE COCOONS are suspended above a podium.
Monique's and Martin's faces are barely visible within their
organic folds, hanging upside down and weeping hysterically.

They hear CHANTING IN NAHUATL, look up to find
Alejandro/Xolotl attired as an Aztec priest of Tlalok,
standing by the cocooned kids. Above dances Kiki/Mictlan,
dressed as a Tlalok too, CHANTING IN NAHUATL.

SAFI'S POV: The six Tzitzimimehs, now prominently visible,
fly and buzz around the cocoons, DRINKING THE KIDS' SUFFERING
AND FEAR, growing progressively brighter.

                    RAFA
               (screams at kiki/Mictlan)
          You! Let them go! What's wrong with
          you, freak?
               (runs to the podium)
          We're here, Monique! Martin! It'll
          be okay!

Kiki/Mictlan waves his hand and the Tzitzimimehs throw Rafa
off, then force the teens to retreat.

                    SAFI
          Watch out!

                    RAFA
               (swiping at his invisible
                attackers)
          Get off me!

Very quickly, both Calian and Rafa are overwhelmed. Rafa
SWEARS, furious.

Safi manages to twist out of the Tzitzimimehs' grip, but
alone, she stands no chance of reaching the cocoons.

                    RAFA (CONT'D)
               (to Safi)
          How do we fight back?!

Safi hesitates.

                    RAFA (CONT'D)
               (swatting)
          We don't have all day here! What do
          you know about them?!

Safi stares at the Tzitzimimehs, flying around the kids,
poking, prodding and otherwise torturing them.

                    SAFI
               (remembers)
          They feed on pain and suffering!

Safi's and Rafa's eyes lock for a moment.

                    SAFI (CONT'D)
          What's the opposite of suffering?

A beat. Suddenly, Safi and Rafa bust out LAUGHING crazily, forcefully, smiling as wide as they can.

And their contrived joy deflects the twitching, cringing Tzitzimimehs!

                    RAFA
          It works! It works!

He rushes at the stage, swinging his arms and LAUGHING. Calian follows, LAUGHING too. As they strike out, CACKLING RAUCOUSLY, the Tzitzimimehs back off, hissing.

                    RAFA (CONT'D)
          I think I hit another one! The dip-
          shits don't like happiness!

Safi and Calian LAUGH, trying to get to the podium --

Rafa COUGHS, too tired to laugh. The Tzitzimimehs attack and strike him, knocking him down. Calian BECOMES HOARSE.

Seeing this, SAFI STARTS SINGING 'AMISH PARADISE' by Weird Al Yankovich.

A beat. Then, Calian and Rafa join in enthusiastically, out of tune and warbling.

It's total chaos and CACOPHONY between the SILLY SONG, the Aztec demon musicians playing their SINISTER MUSIC, and Kiki/Mictlan CHANTING.

Whenever the teens RAISE THEIR VOICES along with the wacky tune, the Tzitzimimehs cringe away, allowing the trio to get nearer to the cocoons.

But as Rafa climbs the podium, Alejandro/Xolotl raises his sacrificial knife and, IN SWIFT CRISS-CROSS MOVEMENTS, SLICES THE COCOONS --

GUTTING MONIQUE AND MARTIN, bound within!

RAFA SCREAMS in blood-curdling horror and the LIGHTS GO OFF.

                    RAFA (O.S.) (CONT'D)
              (screams in the dark)
          Monique! Martin! *No! God, no!*

The light comes back on. Once again, the musicians, Kiki/Mictlan, and Alejandro/Xolotl are gone, and Monique and Martin along with them.

Rafa, Safi, and Calian gawk: there's no blood visible. Instead, candies are strewn all over the podium, spilling from the empty cocoon-like effigies, cut open like pinatas.

                    RAFA (CONT'D)
          Monique! Martin?!
               (weeping)
          Please... please come back. This
          can't be happening!

Calian picks a candy from the floor, unwraps, and licks it.

                    CALIAN
          Hey, I think it was another trick.

                    RAFA
               (howls, to Calian)
          Shut the fuck up!
               (screams through the sobs)
          Kiki! You fucking bitch, if you
          murdered my brother and sister I'll
          rip your ugly head off!

Safi notices a subtle movement in the shadows. She hurries to
its source. Rafa notices and runs after her, with Calian
following shortly behind him.

Safi rounds the temple-stage, sees:

Two Tzitzimimehs dragging the bloody kids aloft. They're
wrapped like mummies, their pale faces visible, eyes closed.
By all accounts, they look dead.

                    SAFI
               (to the Tzitzimimehs)
          Stop! Drop them!
               (swears in Kurdish)
          Bizhi! Kahba!

Rafa and Calian arrive.

RAFA'S POV: the cocoons are being dragged away swiftly by an
invisible force.

                    RAFA
          Son of a bitch!

With Safi hot on their heels, the Tzitzimimehs take off into
the air. Safi jumps up deftly, getting serious air as she
grabs Monique and Martin's feet with each hand.

As the Tzitzimimehs fly up, they carry her along with the two
kids.

Rafa falls behind, screams after her:

                    RAFA (CONT'D)
          Save them, Arab girl! Please!

                    SAFI
              (as she's carried away)
          My name's Safi, and I'm not an
          Arab, dammit!

INT. HAUNTED HOUSE' 'SKY' - CONTINUOUS

They fly through the murky, dark space. The two Tzitzimimehs
struggle to stay airborne, burdened by Safi and the cocoons.

CHITTERING, they try to pull the cocoons in different
directions to force her to drop one of them --

But she pulls back, forcing them to CRASH INTO EACH OTHER in
the air, SCREECHING. They attempt to untangle their rickety
bones from one another.

ANOTHER TZITZIMIMEH flies by and tries to knock Safi off, but
Safi kicks at the demon while LAUGHING hoarsely as she clings
to the cocoons for dear life.

Just then, her TALISMAN slips slightly out of her collar, now
plainly visible --

ONE OF THE ATTACKING TZITZIMIMEHS sees it. Stricken, it
immediately flies off. Another, struggling under the weight
drops the kids and Safi --

Who can't help but let go of the cocoons as she falls,
SCREAMING, through --

The empty darkness of an otherworldly void. Her SCREAM
SOUNDLESS amidst the EPIC SYMPHONIES OF THE SPHERES as the
wrapped kids' bodies tumble through the air next to her.

                                        FADE TO BLACK.

                                        FADE IN:

INT. HELL - CONTINUOUS

Safi opens her eyes, coming to. She scrambles to her feet,
SNIFFS and makes a face. She gawks around, finding:

That she's within an unending, funnel-like space. All is
drenched in gloom around her, save for a small area of the
ground that is illuminated.

She realizes that the patch of light seems to come from her
body. Safi looks down, at her chest -- realizing that her
TALISMAN is GLOWING!

                    SAFI
              (calling out)
          Rafa?! Calian?!

She pulls her blouse collar over her nose to muffle the
stench, then peers around --

A portion of a massive, cavernous space, illuminated only by
GROTESQUE, PHOSPHORESCENT PLANTS. She glances around at
craggy sulfuric rock formations. Mutated slugs, beetles and
arachnoids crawl about amidst streams of molten filth.

                    SAFI (CONT'D)
              Monique?! Martin?!

Suddenly, she trips and stumbles. Upon looking down, she
GASPS, realizing that she's tripped upon --

A mount of human bones, overgrown with gunk protruding here
and there -- a veritable pile of mummified corpses, animal
remains, and detritus.

Her eyes then flit to an even more horrific sight: BLY'S DEAD
BODY, chest raked open, heart torn out.

                    SAFI (CONT'D)
                  (sotto, chanting)
              No, no, no, no...

She backs up only to stumble once more and FALL backwards
directly into --

A PILE OF OTHER BODIES. KEN, CHAD, ERIC, DONALD, SCOTTY,
ANTONIO -- all blood soaked, missing their hearts.

She SHRIEKS IN GUT-WRENCHING TERROR. Bolting to her feet, she
leans over and RETCHES violently.

Once recovered, she jumps at the sound of FOOTSTEPS.

                    VOICE (O.S.)
                  (Spanish accent)
              Hello?! Anyone here?!

Safi gawks at a silhouette stumbling out of the darkness.

REVEAL: It's Enrique. Pale like the walking dead, wild,
sunken eyes staring piercingly at her.

                    SAFI
              Hey, janitor guy! I can't tell you
              how happy I am to see you. What the
              hell is this place?!

                    ENRIQUE
              You said it...

As he moves, his unbuttoned, bloodied shirt opens: his CHEST
is sliced open, heart missing, SPINE visible. She gawks.

ENRIQUE (CONT'D)
Hell. Least I think so.

SAFI
(shuddering, sotto)
How... did you get here?

ENRIQUE
I just woke up here! It was so
dark... then I saw some light --
and found you!

SAFI
I can't believe the underworld
really exists!
(crushed)
Guess that means I'm dead too.

ENRIQUE
No. No, it can't be right. I have
to go home! *Mi madre* will be
worried! She needs me!

SAFI
What's the last thing you remember?

ENRIQUE
I... took a drink... and the
figurine... I was told not to touch
it 'cause it's so fragile, but... I
didn't! I swear! It just fell down
and broke, and this smoke came out
of it, and there was a beetle that
spoke like a... a nasty little
pendejo... and then, nothing!

Safi takes this in.

QUICK FLASHES:

-- She recalls Kiki's spiel:

KIKI/COQUI
... Once the humans were dead and
the fifth sun was gone, he hoped to
turn the whole world into his dark
kingdom, inhabited by monsters
worshipping him. He, a minor god,
would become a supreme ruler of the
universe!

-- Anaya asks Kiki:

                    ANAYA
          What had happened to that figurine?
          The one they trapped him into?

                                        BACK TO:

                    SAFI
               (sotto)
          He must've escaped!

                    ENRIQUE
          Who?

                    SAFI
          Mictlantecuhtli... Mictlan, the god
          of the underworld!
               (thinks fast)
          The Day of the Dead follows
          Halloween... The New Fire is
          approaching. So, he takes in the
          sacrifices performed to other gods.
               (beat, realizes)
          Because he wants to take on their
          powers! To become a supreme ruler
          of a new world!
               (beat, gazes around)
          The world without humans...

Enrique stares at her, not comprehending. They both become
aware of PREDATORY, LOW GROWLS APPROACHING.

Safi's WIDE EYES are locked on Enrique, who trembles in fear.
He steps back, fading into the dark.

She hears a HEAVY STEP, spins toward it, GASPS, and backs off
at the sight of --

AN OVERSIZED, SHAGGY CANINE HEAD, then massive, humanoid
shoulders, and finally, the god XOLOTL steps out of the dark,
a cross between Egyptian god Anubis and a fearsome werewolf.

                    XOLOTL
          Hello, there.

                    SAFI
          You're Xolotl!
               (beat, recognizing his
                voice)
          Wait, aren't you... Kiki's
          assistant? The guy who told me I
          could keep the talisman?!

                    XOLOTL
          The "guy" who told you to get the
          hell out of Mitla!

                    SAFI
          I wanted to, believe me.
               (beat)
          I think I get it now. When Kiki
          told us some of us will be
          detained... she meant, they'd be
          sacrificed!

Xolotl raises his hand, illuminating the grounds with his
glowing palm, clearing the fog around them.

Safi WHIMPERS at the sight of: dead Ken, Bly, Chad, Donald,
Scotty, and Antonio, now joined by also ANOTHER BODY - A
SKINLESS, BLOODY MESS. And then, MONIQUE AND MARTIN, their
little CORPSES stacked atop one another

                    SAFI (CONT'D)
               (sobbing)
          No! They were just children! You
          sick bastard!

She stares at Xolotl in horror.

                    SAFI (CONT'D)
          You're the one who performs the
          rituals for him! _You_ killed them!

                    XOLOTL
          Did you come all the way to look
          for them? Why? They aren't your
          family...
               (at the rest of the
                bodies)
          They aren't your people.

Safi SCREAMS and rushes at him, full of rage. But he easily
grabs her by the upper arms, restraining her.

                    XOLOTL (CONT'D)
          Don't you know that you're special?
          Too special to risk _your_ life for
          those who are not even your
          friends.

                    SAFI
          What's the hell does 'special'
          mean?! Is that why you helped me,
          twice?! I know I saw you- during
          the ball game!
               (beat, realizing)
          'Risk my life?!' So I'm not dead?!

                    XOLOTL
          Maybe not. What if I were to help
          you get out?

                    SAFI
          You mean _out of here_?!

                    XOLOTL
          Better -- out of Mictlan's reach.

                    SAFI
               (thinking fast)
          If I get out, I can get help!
          Calian and Rafa are still stuck
          there!

                    XOLOTL
          Once you're back in the world, I'll
          make sure you won't remember any of
          this, and you won't feel an ounce
          of pain when you hear --
               (at the corpses)
          About them.
               (beat)
          You haven't had an easy go of it.
          Why add more bad memories?

Safi stares at him, terrified, but... ever so tempted.

                    XOLOTL (CONT'D)
          I've observed humans ever since
          they had been created. Time and
          again, they proved themselves
          unworthy. You know what they're
          capable of more than most. Maybe,
          Mictlan is right. They _should_
          return to dust. A new world -- a
          new species -- must arise!

                    SAFI
               (at the surroundings)
          This is your vision? Hell on earth?

                    XOLOTL
          That's unfair. Hell never sees
          itself as hell.
               (beat)
          Just as your world doesn't.

                    SAFI
          You're the twin of Quietzalcoatl.
          How did Mictlan get you to his
          side?!

                    XOLOTL
               (scoffs)
          My twin and the rest of those
          supplicants made me a god of the
          sick and the deformed, the guide of
          the dead.
               (MORE)

                    XOLOTL (CONT'D)
          Gave me all the dirty work they
          preferred not to do themselves.

                    SAFI
          You were Seth too, weren't you? Out
          of all the Egyptian gods, you were
          my dad's favorite!

                    XOLOTL
          Oh, yes. 'The judge.' A fine title,
          but the small-minded humans renamed
          me Satan, and blamed me for their
          own inequities. There is only one
          creature on this earth -- a human
          woman I belong with, nobody else
          matters. And she has only a few
          years left in this world. Whereas
          you, Safi... you belong with no one
          now. Neither of us owes anyone
          anything. You're free from the
          obligations of love. It can be...
          liberating, can it not? What do you
          say?

She stares at the bodies, SIGHS, sadly shakes her head.

                    XOLOTL (CONT'D)
               (gazes at her)
          I have another offer for you then.
          If I could save the two still
          hunted, would you agree to stay?

                    SAFI
          Stay? Here? In hell?! Forever?!

                    XOLOTL
               (cunningly)
          Of course, they wouldn't know about
          your sacrifice... They'll only
          remember that you were a 'rich
          Arab' girl who disappeared.

Safi thinks, crestfallen. She SIGHS, stares at Xolotl.

                    SAFI
          Okay. I'll stay.

He gazes in wonder at her earnest face, grim but determined.

                    XOLOTL
               (smiles)
          You didn't disappoint, my little
          Assyrian waif. I think I'd like to
          get you out of here!

                    SAFI
          What? You're gonna just let me go?
          Go where?!

                    XOLOTL
          Wherever you came from. Back into
          the battle, into the saddle, so to
          speak.

                    SAFI
              (begging re: the corpses)
          But can't you bring them back to
          life?!

                    XOLOTL
          That's not up to me, Safi. I can,
          however, allow you to take their
          bodies -- that's only fair.

                    SAFI
          How am I supposed to carry them?!

Safi GASPS in wonder as, abruptly, the teens and the kids'
bodies shrink -- TURNING INTO KACHINAS! The kachinas then
levitate off the ground --

-- Safi's backpack unzips of its own accord and the kachinas
'stream' in, the zipper closing behind them.

She looks at Xolotl. HIS DOG-FACE suddenly looms huge, right
before hers. Everything starts to spin around, until only
darkness remains and his voice becomes all-consuming.

                    XOLOTL (V.O.)
          Keep your talisman hidden, it can
          only protect one!

INT. 'PINATAS' HALL' - CONTINUOUS

Safi opens her eyes, sits up. Surprised to find that she's
alone. She gets up, shoulders her backpack, feels the
talisman under her shirt. She calls out:

                    SAFI
          Rafa! Calian!

                    RAFA (O.S.)
              (not too distant)
          Safi!

Safi hurries toward his voice.

INT. PASSAGE - CONTINUOUS

She rounds the corner and bumps headlong into RAFA.

                    RAFA (CONT'D)
          My brother and sister!.. where are
          they?!

Calian catches up.

                    SAFI
          It's... I...

She's unable to bring herself to tell him. Just then:

                    ANAYA (O.S.)
          Calian?! Help! I'm so scared!

The three exchange looks and hurry toward the voice.

INT. CAGE ROOM - CONTINUOUS

They run in to see:

Anaya, trapped in a small cage, still clad in the bulky
ritual clothing she danced in --

                    ANAYA (CONT'D)
          Let me out!

Gobsmacked, they rush to free Anaya.

                    CALIAN
          But... you got your head cut off!

Anaya climbs out of the cage.

NOTE: throughout the following scenes with Anaya, she
pointedly avoids standing too close to the rest of the teens.

                    ANAYA
          Just special effects. Pretty
          impressive ones.

                    RAFA
          What about Martin and Monique?! Do
          you know what they did with them?

                    ANAYA
          No, but Kiki said that the kids are
          fine. And the guys are too.

                    RAFA
               (exhales in relief)
          Thank God. Or... Gods.
               (beat)
          We still should sue that freak-show
          motherfucker, though.

Safi watches Anaya closely.

                    SAFI
               (to Anaya)
          Why'd you ask Kiki about the kids?!
          They were still with us when you
          disappeared!

                    ANAYA
          I... actually didn't. I asked him
          about the guys. He said they were
          good and the kids too! They'll
          catch up after this last challenge
          and we can all go home.

Safi stares at Anaya in subtle disbelief.

                    CALIAN
               (perks up)
          What kinda challenge?

                    ANAYA
          The kind that if you get through,
          they'll broadcast the video all
          over the internet! It'll go viral!
          And you won't believe the reward!

                    CALIAN
               (eager)
          Oh yeah?!

                    ANAYA
          It's like this really cool
          scholarship. They said, you can get
          into any college you want! But
          let's get real... you're the only
          one who can win this, Calian.
          You're, like, the one true warrior!

                    RAFA
          Is that your opinion, Anaya, or has
          your friend Kiki already decided on
          a winner?

Anaya ignores this.

                    CALIAN
               (to Rafa and Safi, happy)
          Man, this is one wild spot!

Anaya walks ahead, turns to them, waiting.

                    ANAYA
          C'mon, guys! Let's just finish
          this! We can't get out anyway!

                    SAFI
          How'd you get into that cage?

                    ANAYA
          I dunno... One minute I was
          dancing, then the next I was all
          scrunched up behind the bars. That
          Kiki is a horrible practical joker,
          but pretty damn genius.

                    SAFI
          So Kiki and Xolotl stuffed you into
          there?!

                    ANAYA
               (sharply)
          How do you know his name?

                    SAFI
          Whose? The old guy's?
               (beat, fibbing)
          I just gave him a nickname. His
          face sorta reminds of a dog, or a
          wolf... right?

Anaya gazes at Safi, then turns and hurries out. They rush
after her.

INT. VARIOUS PASSAGES - CONTINUOUS

Scary exhibits pop up in their way -- among them, a SPLIT-IN-
TWO SIAMESE TWIN DUMMY jumps at Anaya, howling all the while.
She dodges it expertly.

                    SAFI (CONT'D)
          You didn't squeal that time!

                    ANAYA
          Why should I?! I'm no sissy moron.

                    RAFA
          That's a change.

                    CALIAN
          Pipe down, dickwad.

                    SAFI
               (to Rafa, sotto)
          You don't buy that _everything_ we
          saw is fake, do you?!

He lurches away from a dummy zombie knight with a papier-
mache sword.

                    RAFA
          All _these_ are pretty fake...

                    SAFI
               (sotto)
     Now they are! Since she showed up!
     What about the Tzitzimimehs?!

                    RAFA
     You know, it *is* just way too
     convenient that only girls can see
     them.
               (to Anaya)
     Hey! Did you see those...
     Tzitzimimeh things?

                    SAFI
     The shimmering skeletons, Anaya,
     remember?!

                    ANAYA
               (glances back at them)
     Actually, I don't think so.
     Something shimmered. I don't know
     what it was.

                    SAFI
     That's not true, Anaya! You *did* see
     them! I saw you looking at them!
     Why are you lying?

                    ANAYA
     Excuse me? Maybe *you're* the liar?

                    RAFA
     There definitely was something. It
     fought us, we all felt it! And
     something carried my brother and
     sister away. I saw it.

                    SAFI
     It's not just the Tzitzimimehs!
     Listen... this is hard to explain,
     but these things that we saw...
     they were real, okay? Mictlan, the
     god of the dead, escaped. He wants
     to collect the other gods' powers,
     so he performs sacrifices to them
     and eats the hearts himself! We
     need to get out of here!

Anaya stares at Safi.

                    ANAYA
     Where'd you get all that from?!

                    CALIAN
          She's an Aztec expert, duh. She
          keeps coming up with these wild
          stories.

                    ANAYA
          We can't get out until the game is
          over. Kiki told me that,
          specifically. And Safi, you're
          smart and all... but that doesn't
          mean you can just _invent_ all that
          stuff to get attention!

Safi simmers, pissed.

                    RAFA
               (to Safi)
          Kiki is a bitch, for sure, but
          Anaya is alive, even though we _saw_
          her head cut off -- so her story
          sounds legit. If we need to finish
          the stupid game to get my brother
          and sister back, that's what we're
          gonna do.

Off Safi's torn look, they enter a --

INT. COMBAT ROOM - CONTINUOUS

A towering, primal space with another, even more impressive
replica of an actual Aztec temple in the center.

                    CALIAN
          Sheesh...

Anaya hurries to the bottom of the temple, spots what looks
like a giant boulder, with metal loops sticking out of it.

                    ANAYA
          That's the last challenge! A
          champion has to fight while tied
          up!
               (coyly, looks at Calian)
          Ready for greatness, prince Calian?

                    RAFA
          Oh, it's his show now? Good.

                    CALIAN
               (enthusiastic)
          Ready as ever. But I need a weapon!

                    ANAYA
          On it!

She reaches behind a fake bush nearby and pulls out an actual
replica of Aztec broad sword and gives it to him.

                    RAFA
               (at the sword)
          How'd you know that was there?!

                    ANAYA
          Miss Kiki told me.

Calian ties a rope to his own ankle, making sure that it's
secure. He next ties the other end to a metal loop in the
boulder. Then strikes a heroic poses with the sword.

                    CALIAN
          Are they putting it on Youtube?!
          How about TikTok?

                    ANAYA
          Yeah, Instagram too!

                    SAFI
               (to Anaya)
          So, I know Kiki told you that
          everybody is okay and safe.
               (to the three)
          But I'm telling you all they're
          not!

          ANAYA   RAFA
Oh, really, Safi? And what   (worried again)
did happen to them, then?   What do you mean?

                    SAFI
          I... look, you've got to believe
          me. We're all in danger!

                    ANAYA
          You know what I think? I think
          you're a coward, like all Arabs!
          You grew up filthy rich from oil
          and you're used to being admired.
          So now you lie to be the center of
          attention.

                    SAFI
               (to Anaya)
          But I told _you_ that I'm not rich,
          and not an Arab! _You_ know my story!
          How can you say that...
               (at Calian and Rafa)
          Please, listen to me!

                    ANAYA
               (also to the boys)
          I'm tired of this attention whore.
               (MORE)

                    ANAYA (CONT'D)
          If you two want to run away like
          little bitches when you're so close
          to the prize, be my guests. I'm
          staying!

                    RAFA
          Wow, Anaya. I never thought you
          were that ballsy.

                    ANAYA
          So, what it gonna be? Me or her?!

Her lips trembling, Safi stares at Calian and Rafa in turns.

                    RAFA
               (to Safi)
          Let's be real, your story _is_ kinda
          nutty...

Safi is shaken, but holds her head high.

                    ANAYA
               (sweetly, to Safi)
          Don't feel bad. This whole venue
          was really designed for those with
          native blood...

                    SAFI
               (mocks)
          Venue. _Venue?_ I heard you before...
          you didn't talk like that, and now
          suddenly, you're like...
               (searches for words, mad)
          A socialite or something!

                    ANAYA
          Ah, Safi! Just go kneel on a prayer
          rug somewhere and leave us be,
          would you? You're not really one of
          us.

                    SAFI
          That's just fine by me!
               (bitterly, to them all)
          You know what?! I don't want to be
          one of you! You're selfish, and...
          close-minded... and stupid! If you
          don't want to listen to the one
          person who's trying to help you,
          then go right ahead!

Safi turns on her heels and walks toward the door. Rafa looks
after her, frowning.

                    RAFA
          Safi! Come on!

But she keeps going. Then, on the way to the entrance, Safi
slows down, stricken by pangs of conscience.

                              QUICK FLASHES:

-- Safi and Calian playing together in the Aztec ball game.

-- Rafa and Safi, fighting side by side.

-- Rafa screaming after her, as the Tzitzimimehs carry her
away.

-- Xolotl's WOLF FACE, while in hell:

                    XOLOTL
          Keep your talisman hidden, it can
          only protect one!

                              BACK TO:

About to exit, Safi SIGHS... and turns back in time to see:

From above, papier-mache JAGUAR AND EAGLE EFFIGIES swoop down
and attack Calian. He SCREAMS like an Apache warrior and
springs to fight them.

CALIAN POV: he cannot see the real attackers, swings after
the effigies with reckless abandon. His sword is wooden and
dull, but he manages to break off the Jaguar's ear and tail,
and the Eagle's leg.

                    CALIAN
          Take that! I'm the greatest!

                    SAFI
          Stop, stop it!
               (to Rafa and Anaya)
          Untie him!

                    ANAYA
               (groans, annoyed)
          Oh my gosh, can't you just go
          away?!

Calian slashes one of the eagle's wing off. The effigies keep
on fighting even though partially dismembered and hobbled. He
dodges the jaguar's claws:

                    CALIAN
               (screams victoriously)
          Booyah! How you like me now!?
               (to Safi)
          Don't kill the vibe!

                    SAFI
          Listen to me! They tied warriors up
          for a fake fight before sacrificing
          them to Tezcatlipoca!

Calian slashes off one of the jaguar's legs:

                    CALIAN
          Chill! This is just a game! These
          things aren't alive.

                    SAFI
          They're controlled by the
          Tzitzimimehs!

Anaya scowls at her darkly.

                    ANAYA
          Crazy, deluded sand-camel.

Anaya turns away from Safi, watching Calian with glowing
eyes. Rafa stares at Anaya, uncertain.

Safi sees something on the ground: dark droplets. She reaches
and smudges one on her finger -- it's blood!

                                        QUICK FLASH:

The bloody, skinless body in the underworld.

                                        BACK TO:

A light bulb moment for Safi. Now, she sees --

That Anaya is looking directly... no, she's actually controls
the Tzitzimimehs with small movements!

Safi peers at the ground, spots more blood drops in Anaya's
wake. She sneakily approaches Rafa while Anaya is distracted,
points at the blood drops.

                    RAFA
          Ew! Someone's on the rag.

                    SAFI
              (to Rafa, quiet)
          No, dummy. Whenever they beheaded a
          girl to sacrifice her to Coatlicue,
          they would skin her, and the priest
          would wear her skin!
              (to Anaya, loudly)
          Why are you so pale, Anaya? And how
          come you're still wearing that
          Coatlicue costume?

Anaya turns her head slowly, to glare at Safi.

Rafa stares at her... his eyes drift to -- Anaya's real hands hanging like mittens from under the bulky costume. His eyes widen in realization.

He moves quickly, bolting forward and YANKING ANAYA'S SKIN CLEAN OFF, revealing --

A blood-smeared Kiki/Mictlan underneath! Anaya's de-boned, bloody remains fall under his feet in a sloppy heap.

Rafa jumps away, horrified.

                    RAFA
          You... you motherfucker!

Calian stumbles and falls on his backside, totally shocked.

                    CALIAN
               (sotto)
          No way.

Given a window, the Jaguar LUNGES, BITING a chunk out of Calian's forearm as the latter SHRIEKS IN PAIN.

                    RAFA
               (at Kiki)
          What did you do to my sister and
          brother?! My friends! _Where are_
          they!?

Before Kiki/Mictlan can respond, Safi has to pipe up:

                    SAFI
          They're... they're dead, Rafa. I'm
          so, so sorry.

Rafa is absolutely devastated. Rocked beyond words. A beat.

                    RAFA
          You knew this whole time... and you
          didn't tell me?

                    SAFI
          I couldn't. I couldn't find the
          right words... and moment to... So
          sorry ---

                    KIKI/MICTLAN
          Enough talk!
               (rubbing his stomach)
          I hunger.

                    RAFA
               (howls to Calian)
          Give me that sword!

He reaches for the sword, only for it to instantly --

TRANSFORM INTO A GIANT FEATHER.

Kiki/Mictlan signals, and the Tzitzimimehs drop the animal effigies, which shatter on impact around battered Calian. The entities then attack Rafa and Safi.

Rafa grabs the papier-mache eagle's wing from the ground and Safi grabs another. They use them to take swings at the Tzitzimimehs, keeping them at bay.

A couple Tzitzimimeh attack Calian, armed only with the worthless feather. Still on the ground, he attempts to scare them off with LAUGHTER, but is too hoarse.

He SCREAMS as they cut him with their sharp, bony fingers.

                    CALIAN
          Help me, guys!

Safi and Rafa try to fight their way toward him.

SAFI POV: amidst the chaos, Alejandro/Xolotl -- again in his human form -- walks out on top of the pyramid, dressed as a priest of Tezcatlipoca. He stares impassively at her.

                    KIKI/MICTLAN
          (to Alejandro/Xolotl)
          Will you be able to destroy the
          blood of your old master? That
          would be the best way to transfer
          his power... and your allegiance to
          me, once and for all!

Calian curls into a ball on the ground, whimpers at the attacking Tzitzimimehs:

                    CALIAN
          Leave me alone, please!

                    KIKI/MICTLAN
          (to Calian, roars)
          Get up! Be worthy of the great
          Aztec kings, your ancestors! Your
          heart must be full of courage as
          you die!

                    CALIAN
          Aztec ancestors?! My dad is Hopi!

                    KIKI/MICTLAN
          (impatient)
          ... Your mother, then. She must be
          a descendant of Huitzilopochtli!
                    (MORE)

                    KIKI/MICTLAN (CONT'D)
          That's how you got your beautiful
          Aztec face!

                    CALIAN
          My mother is Korean! *Ouch!*

                    KIKI/MICTLAN
               (thunders)
          What?!

Kiki/Mictlan snatches the knife from Alejandro/Xolotl,
adroitly glide-jumps over Calian, then smells him closely.

                    KIKI/MICTLAN (CONT'D)
          You're not of Huitzu's blood!

                    CALIAN
          Told you! Can I go?

Instead, Kiki/Mictlan slashes open Calian's chest, RIPS OUT
his HEART and BITES through it like an apple!

Safi and Rafa SCREAM. Kiki/Mictlan turns to them, eyeing Rafa
as the teens back off.

                    KIKI/MICTLAN
               (to Rafa)
          You... It must be you, then! No
          wonder you survived for so long!
          You must be the one I smelt all
          along -- the true descendant of the
          great Huitzu!

He signals to the Tzitzimimehs and throws the sacrificial
knife to Alejandro/Xolotl, who catches it.

The six Tzitzimimehs rush at Rafa and Safi, who press their
backs to each other in an attempt to ward them off.

                    KIKI/MICTLAN (CONT'D)
          Ah! That's more like it! He fights
          like a true warrior.

The talisman glows under Safi's shirt, holding the
Tzitzimimehs at bay. But they manage to grab Rafa.

                    SAFI
          No!

The winged beings carry a struggling Rafa to the stage of the
temple. Safi rushes after them.

                    KIKI/MICTLAN
               (to Rafa)
          Rejoice, your noble heart will make
          me a supreme ruler!

SAFI'S POV: Rafa is dropped onto a slab. The Tzitzimimehs
spring to tie him down. She rushes to him.

Kiki/Mictlan lets go of the knife- and it flies into
Alejandro/Xolotl's hand.

                    KIKI/MICTLAN (CONT'D)
                (to Alejandro/Xolotl)
            You're up, old man!

Alejandro/Xolotl unhurriedly approaches the slab. He
theatrically raises the knife to strike. But as the blade's
about to plunge down --

Safi reaches the top and throws herself on top of bound Rafa!

                    SAFI
                (to Alejandro/Xolotl)
            Don't! Please!

The Tzitzimimehs rush at her and Rafa again, but her talisman
GLOWS UNDER HER SHIRT, warding them off. Alejandro/Xolotl
stares down at her and Rafa.

Then, he lowers the knife.

                    KIKI/MICTLAN
                (to Alejandro/Xolotl)
            Dispose of her! What are you
            waiting for?!

Alejandro/Xolotl doesn't move while Safi hurriedly unties
Rafa. One of the TZITZIMIMEHS swoops in and LATCHES on to her
from behind, ripping her backpack off.

It unzips and some of the Kachinas spill out. Kiki/Mictlan is
taken aback.

                    KIKI/MICTLAN (CONT'D)
            How did you get those?
                (glares at
                 Alejandro/Xolotl)
            You... you always were a
            sentimental fool!

He swoops toward the teens, but an ANIMALISTIC GROWL rings
out as --

Alejandro/Xolotl morphs into his wolf form and jumps in
Kiki/Mictlan's way, shielding Safi. Rafa whimpers, cowering.

                    KIKI/MICTLAN (CONT'D)
                (laughing, incredulous)
            No, you senile buffoon, I won't
            fight you. You forgot, I hold the
            trump card!

He signals to the Tzitzimimehs. A few fly off, Xolotl's wolf
eyes following them anxiously.

Simultaneously, Rafa leaps down from the slab.

RAFA'S POV: he notices that one of the Kachinas looks exactly
like Monique. He grabs it, stares at it, then sees another
that looks like Martin, grabs it too.

The Tzitzimimehs drag in disheveled, resisting Isobel.

                    ISOBEL
          Keep your hands off me, bony
          bitches!

They drop her. She gets up, peers around, bewildered. Her
eyes land on Xolotl and she GASPS in terror.

                    KIKI/MICTLAN
          (laughing)
          So much for love being blind! I
          always said, nobody ever knows or
          loves us for who we really are!

                    ISOBEL
          Oh, my gods! Is that...

She stares as if she can't look away, walks up to Xolotl. He
looks back at her as if hypnotized.

                    ISOBEL (CONT'D)
          Alejandro?! Is that you?

She approaches him, looks up into his vulpine face.

                    ISOBEL (CONT'D)
          You always reminded me of a wolf! I
          wish I knew you really were one.

                    XOLOTL
          You mean... you're not repulsed by
          me?

                    ISOBEL
          (caresses his snout)
          Why would I be? Married to the
          great Xolotl?! I'm the luckiest gal
          alive!

                    KIKI/MICTLAN
          (can't help piping in)
          You should see _me_ in my full
          regalia! I'm great Mictlantecuhtli,
          the god of death -- and soon, of
          the whole world!

                    ISOBEL
              (to Mictlan, sarcastic)
          Of course you are!
              (to Xolotl)
          What does that *hijo de puta* want?

                    XOLOTL
              (at Rafa and Safi)
          To kill those kids... and to
          destroy the world.

ANGLE ON: behind them, unnoticed, Rafa hurriedly gathers the
fallen Kachinas into the backpack.

                    ISOBEL
          So, those tall tales you've told me
          weren't tales... they were stories
          of your past!

She kisses his furry cheek, whispers:

                    ISOBEL (CONT'D)
          We had a good life, *mi amor*. Let
          our hearts bring back your brother!

A tear runs down his snout. Isobel nods at Safi and Rafa,
standing side by side as Rafa holds her backpack to his
chest:

                    ISOBEL (CONT'D)
          They look good together. Almost as
          good as we did.

Their eyes lock for a moment. Then, Xolotl HOWLS and --

Plunges the knife into Isobel's chest.

Safi and Rafa SCREAM. Xolotl tears loose Isobel's heart as
she falls.

He then plunges the knife into his own chest. Everybody
stares transfixed as --

His glowing heart floats out into the air of its own accord
and Isobel's joins it.

The talisman slips from under Safi's shirt collar and glows
in response. Kiki/Mictlan sees it. Suddenly, there's --

A HEARTBEAT. Another HEARTBEAT joins it. AND ANOTHER.

REVEAL: it's Kiki/Mictlan's chest that pulsates with the
manifold HEARTBEATS, the hearts trying to get out! He whacks
hard against his breastbone to shut them up, snaps to Safi:

                         KIKI/MICTLAN
                        (at the talisman)
                 Where did you get it?! Who did you
                 steal it from?!

He swoops forth, grabbing fallen Xolotl's knife.

The two hearts float toward Safi. Kiki/Mictlan races to
intercept them, but they slip through his grasp.

The Tzitzimimehs attempt to grab the hearts, only to hiss and
fly off as if burned upon contact.

As Kiki/Mictlan races to get to Safi and Rafa before the
hearts do --

Safi thrusts the talisman at him as Rafa hides behind her.
The talisman's energy barely holds Kiki/Mictlan back. He
LAUGHS, raises his dagger.

                      KIKI/MICTLAN (CONT'D)
                 Not good enough, I'm afraid.

Right as he's about to stab, the two hearts evade the
Tzitzimimehs and dart into the talisman, fusing energies.

It BURSTS into an incandescent ball of golden light. Safi
SCREAMS as it sinks into her chest cavity, fusing with her
own heart. Her whole body arches and glows brightly.

Rafa SHRIEKS as if burned. He tries to let go but is unable
to, his palms glued to Safi.

Kiki/Mictlan SQUEALS, dropping the knife. Time itself FREEZES
as we --

                                             SLAM TO:

EXT. SPIRIT DIMENSION - CONTINUOUS

They finds themselves -- Safi as a participant, Rafa as a an
observer -- in a strange space filled with radiance.

It bends and distorts Safi's form as she turns into a ball of
light that brings us into --

                                             FLASHBACK:

EXT. SYRIAN REFUGEE CAMP - CONTINUOUS

An air strike wreaks fiery havoc on the refugee camp.
EXPLOSIONS and SCREAMS intermingle. Tents burn while MEN with
firehoses try to put out blazes.

Bodies are covered and carried away past a WAILING, a bit younger Safi, kneeling by her DEAD PARENTS.

Suddenly, present-Safi's ORB beams into frame, turning a scene of unimaginable darkness into one of BEAMING LIGHT which brings us --

                                        BACK TO:

                    RAFA
          You're a refugee!

He looks up to find Safi's gone.

                    SAFI (V.O.)
          What's happening? What am I? *Where*
          am I?!

INT. ETHER DIMENSION - CONTINUOUS

A glowing "road" of DNA strands. The ball of light/Safi travels along it, back and back, landing as --

A glowing fetus in her mother's belly. Then jumping further into her paternal GRANDMOTHER, before continuing along --

THE TOPSY-TURVY DNA STRANDS, SUSPENDED IN SPACE, 'JUMPING' FROM ONE ANCESTOR TO THE PREVIOUS ONE, THROUGHOUT HISTORY.

                    XOLOTL (V.O.)
          Souls travel along the bloodlines!
          Every part of you came from someone
          else. You're made of the soul
          particles of your ancestors. You
          know everything they knew, even if
          you're not aware of it, and you had
          experienced everything they lived
          through, even if you don't remember
          it.

The blue spark keeps on hopping along the 'road' as centuries and millenniums pass by before finally landing on --

A proud young couple in ANCIENT EGYPT. Royal Captain TALEC and his elegant wife TIA, who looks almost Aztec. He clutches her pregnant belly lovingly.

                    XOLOTL (V.O.)
          So that's how it happened...

                                        ENTER ANIMATION
                                        SEQUENCE:

-- Talec is on board an ancient Egyptian trading vessel as it carries him across the ocean, to the coast of South America.

> XOLOTL (V.O.)
> A few thousand years ago, noble
> young Talec, the captain of the
> pharaoh's merchant fleet, visited
> the kingdom of the Olmecs... whose
> royal family and gods later became
> those of the Aztecs. Apparently,
> while trading, Talec fell in love
> with Tia, the Olmec princess, who
> received a whopping portion of
> Huitzu blood from her mother...

-- A blue glow resonates about Tia's head as Talec and she
are married by an OLMEC PRIEST on top of a resplendent
pyramid temple. Tia's MOTHER sports a similar blue glow
around her head.

-- Back onto the 'DNA road.' From Tia's mother, the light
jumps onto a previous QUEEN, then into the ONE BEFORE THAT,
concentrating and becoming brighter with every jump until --

-- Ultimately landing upon the familiar, giant, radiant ALIEN
FIGURE. At his/her side stands the much smaller figure of his
EARTHLING WIFE. Behind them in the distance, the sleek SPACE
CRAFT looms.

> SAFI (V.O.)
> Huitzilopochtli!

> XOLOTL (V.O.)
> An immortal, multidimentional, bi-
> gendered, bi-sexual being with
> magical powers stranded in Earth.
> Same as the rest of those you call
> 'gods' who seeded the humanity with
> its first royal dynasties.

                                        END MONTAGE.

The ball of energy BEAMS back into the room before spinning
and flipping about frantically. It then momentarily expands
back into the form of --

Safi, who gasps as light beams through her every pore down to
the cellular level, blasting in all directions as she
transforms into --

Huitzilopochtli himself, raising the talisman as it morphs
into a SLITHERING, GLITTERING SERPENT... THEN INTO A SWORD OF
LIGHT.

> KIKI/MICTLAN
> (stunned)
> Huitzu?!

                    SAFI/HUITZILOPOCHTLI
          The Mesopotamian edition,
          motherfucker!

Safi/Huizilopochtli raises her sword of light, and throws it
at Kiki/Mictlan --

Who dodges it, and flies up, growing in size, spinning like a
firecracker and emitting rapid sparks which quickly set the
surrounding area ablaze.

Safi -- now back to her normal shape and size but glowing
slightly -- and Rafa grab Calian's body, and carry it running
out of the hall.

Mictlan rages high above them, the sword of light flying
after him, hot on his tail.

<u>INT. MUSEUM - CONTINUOUS</u>

The fire spreads rapidly through the museum, accompanied by a
noxious green smoke. Safi and Rafa cough and hack, wheezing
for air. It appears that all hope is lost.

Just then, they see the 'Bony & Clyde' car. Raga hurries to
it.

                    SAFI
          Careful!

                    RAFA
          It's not Aztec! C'mon!

He pulls the two dummies out.

                    RAFA (CONT'D)
          You still got some of that 'god
          power?!'

                    SAFI
          I'm not sure...

                    RAFA
          Only one way to find out. Come on!

They hurriedly lay Calian's body on the back seat. Safi gets
in while Rafa leaps into the passenger seat, taking off the
backpack and holding it on his lap.

Safi lays her glowing hands onto the steering wheel. She
closes her eyes, concentrates. Nothing happens.

                    RAFA (CONT'D)
          I know you can do it!

Safi shuts her eyes, FOCUSES --

And with that, the car ROARS to life.

                    RAFA (CONT'D)
          Yes!

They take off, zooming through the burning building, Safi
driving while Rafa screams warnings and directions.

The car veers around corners as the walls sprout eyes and
clawed tentacles that reach out for their vehicle.

Bony snake spines slither through the car, attempting to hold
it back. Safi SWERVES harshly to the right, severing loose
the spines and tentacles. High above, in the --

MYSTIC 'SKIES'

The serpent sword pursues Kiki/Mictlan. He dodges and weaves,
but finally --

It catches up with him and STABS into his chest, tearing him
open in one fell swoop.

Kiki/Mictlan SCREAMS as all the hearts he had consumed shoot
out of him within beams of light. He spews green smoke and
deflates like a punctured balloon as he spins earthbound.

IN THE CAR

The hearts hit the vehicle like lightening bolts, jumping in
through the windows. Rafa HOLLERS and throws the backpack to
the back seat, where it promptly catches fire and --

The kachinas fall out. One of the shooting star hearts
plunges into Calian's gaping chest and --

He STIRS, awakened.

                    CALIAN
          Hey... where am I?!

Other 'shooting' hearts enter the kachinas and the car
careens, nearly spinning out as it SHATTERS THROUGH THE GLASS
ENTRANCE OF THE LOBBY --

EXT. MUSEUM - CONTINUOUS

SCREAMS erupt as the car comes to a jerky halt. A loaded
beat. Then:

The doors fling open and *all the sacrificed teens, as well as
Monique and Martin*, come tumbling out of it, overflowing the
cramped vehicle.

                    TEENS
          Hey, move!/ Ow, my back!/ Sorry!/
          You squashed me!/ Come on, dude!

As a portion of the museum is consumed by flames, POLICE AND
FIRE TRUCK SIRENS become audible in the distance.

ANGLE ON: Safi hovers within a bubble of eerie light
alongside a shimmering Xolotl. Watching it all.

                    XOLOTL
          They won't remember anything they
          shouldn't.

                    SAFI
          What if I tell them?

Xolotl just looks at her.

                    SAFI (CONT'D)
          Right... I wouldn't believe me
          either.

                                        CUT TO:

INT. MUSEUM - CONTINUOUS

A HEART soars through the billowing smoke and raging
conflagration like a guided missile, aiming straight for --

The PRONE BODY OF MS. ROMERO. It plunges into her gaping
bloody chest and she --

GASPS awake. Staring about at the flaming chaos, bewildered.
Her wound has disappeared.

                    MS. ROMERO
          Lord have mercy... what's
          happening!?

Then, a DARK SHAPE appears behind her, drawing nearer. She
whips around just in time to --

REVEAL: it's a FIREFIGHTER emerging from the smoke. He helps
her to her feet and carries her out.

ANGLE ON: some distance away, a beautiful, glowing blue heart
enters dead Kiki's chest. She rapidly scrambles up to her
feet, calls around hectically:

                    KIKI/COQUI
          Xonaxi! Xonaxi!

EXT. MUSEUM - CONTINUOUS

<u>IN THE EERIE BUBBLE:</u> Safi and Xolotl watch THE TOURISTS AND
VISITORS gather.

The dazed teens try to regain their bearings. Calian consoles
Anaya. Ms. Romero shows up and runs to them. Much hugging and
comforting ensues. Enrique staggers around, confused.

> SAFI
> (deflated)
> So everything's back to what it was
> before? Everything?!

> XOLOTL
> Not quite.

PUFF! Xolotl disappears, the eerie bubble along with him.

Safi finds herself standing alone. Rafa approaches:

> RAFA
> Hey, I just wanted to say... Ah,
> never mind, I'm no good with words.

Safi's eyes widen as he hugs her tight. As they part, Monique
and Martin approach, all smiles.

> MONIQUE AND MARTIN
> Thank you, Safi, for getting us out
> of the fire!

> RAFA
> Yeah. What they said.

> SAFI
> (unsure)
> You're, um, welcome...

Donald approaches.

> DONALD
> What the hell happened back there?

> RAFA
> The last thing I saw before the
> fire broke out was Anaya dancing...

Rafa scratches his head, confused. Safi realizes that he
didn't remember the final battle with Mictlan.

> DONALD
> I think, we were playing some weird
> ball game and then... *bam!* Flames
> all around!

                    RAFA
          It's all that smoke, probably made
          us black out. But I remember who
          helped me get loose.
                    (beat, to Safi)
          Mom and I wanted to talk to you...

Ms. Romero, after being given the all-clear by a MEDIC,
hurries to them, smiles at Safi.

                    MS. ROMERO
                    (to Rafa)
          Did you ask her?

                    RAFA
          I was about to.

                    SAFI
          Ask me what?

                    MS. ROMERO
          Safi, Rafa and Anaya told me about
          your situation. We're wondering if
          you would like to... come to live
          with us? I've hosted some foster
          kids before...

Safi stares at them. Heartened, yet torn.

                    SAFI
          I'm... very grateful for your
          offer. But...

                    RAFA
          We live on a pueblo. And we're not
          rich. My mom's a teacher, and my
          dad...
                    (beat)
          He's not around. But we still have
          a nice life.

                    SAFI
          It's not about that. See, I'm kind
          of a fugitive now. I've stolen a
          car, and an ID, and almost four
          hundred dollar, and might've,
          well... injured someone pretty
          bad...
                    (hurriedly)
          But he was a bad man! I would never
          have done those things if I didn't
          have to.

Rafa and Ms. Romero exchange a glance.

                    RAFA
          We believe you.

                    MS. ROMERO
               (smiles)
          I think maybe your troubles are not
          as bad as you think they are, Safi.
          You just need a little help to
          navigate the system.

                    RAFA
          And we can help her with that,
          right, mom?

                    MS. ROMERO
          We can and we will!

Safi smiles broadly.

EXT. BACK AREA OF MUSEAM - CONTINUOUS

SCREAMING, a greatly reduced Mictlan falls from the sky,
landing with a thud. He's now little more than a child-sized,
bloated man-frog with a distended stomach.

                    XANA/XONAXI (O.S.)
          Look at you, honey!

He turns to find Xana/Xonaxi and Kiki/Coqui, standing next to
each another, waiting for him like a welcoming committee.

                    XANA/XONAXI (CONT'D)
               (to Mictlan)
          Back to your proper form!

                    MICTLAN
               (in a squeaky voice)
          How dare you mock me! I'm your
          husband and ruler!

                    KIKI/COQUI
          Ah, slimy one, this is *so* fifteen
          hundreds!

                    MICTLAN
               (roars/squeaks)
          You treacherous slags!

They pretend to be scared, cowed, and pressing to each other
as he bares his fangs and rushes at them. At the last moment,
they step apart, revealing a steel container between them --

Mictlan flies headlong into it and his ex-wives promptly shut
it. It glows red and shakes as he rages inside.

Kiki taps it and it becomes still, then shrinks to a hand-
held size, which Xana stuffs into her purse.

                    XANA/XONAXI
          Works every time! Hopefully, this
          one will hold him.

                    KIKI/COQUI
          Humans have plenty of their own
          overambitious demons to contend
          with.

                    XANA/XONAXI
          Yes, but those aren't our
          responsibility!

The two walk off.

INT. THE LIGHT-FILLED, SPIRIT REALM - LATER

Xolotl and Isobel look through a glistening window into the
mortal world, showing:

INT. PUEBLO HIGH SCHOOL - CAFETERIA - DAY

Where Safi, Calian, Rafa, Anaya, and the rest of the jocks
have lunch together, teasing each other.

                    ISOBEL (O.S.)
               Will they manage?

                    XOLOTL (O.S.)
          The leader has found his priestess.
          They have a fighting chance now.

We GLIDE IN ON: Rafa and Safi laughing. Their spirits high.
Happy together.

                                        FADE TO BLACK.